HIT MEN DON'T TAKE CREDIT CARDS

HIT MEN DON'T TAKE CREDIT CARDS

JENNIFER L. WHITE

ARCHWAY
PUBLISHING

This is a work of fiction. All of the characters, names, incidents, organizations, and dialogue in this novel are either the products of the author's imagination or are used fictitiously.

Archway Publishing books may be ordered through booksellers or by contacting:

Archway Publishing
1663 Liberty Drive
Bloomington, IN 47403
www.archwaypublishing.com
844-669-3957

ISBN: 978-1-6657-5531-3 (sc)
ISBN: 978-1-6657-5529-0 (hc)
ISBN: 978-1-6657-5530-6 (e)

Library of Congress Control Number: 2024900532

Print information available on the last page.

Archway Publishing rev. date: 02/22/2024

ABOUT THE AUTHOR

Jennifer L. White lives in Webster Groves, MO, a suburb of St. **Louis, MO**. Born in Louisiana, Jennifer graduated from Louisiana State University in 1986 with a degree in Journalism. Subsequently, she moved to Atlanta, GA where she worked for a medical publishing company and then for a national nonprofit fundraising organization in Atlanta as a Vice President. In Atlanta, Jennifer suffered a massive brain stem stroke and was given a a 4% survival rate by her surgeon. On route to the emergency room via abulance she lost the function of all her organs and was resuscitated. After an 8 month stint in a local Atlanta, GA rehab facility, Jennifer moved with her husband to Springfield, MO where she had a number of editorials published in the newspaper and eventually wrote this book. The hemorrhagic stroke that she experienced at 36 years old (23 years ago) made her unable to work as she once did so she is currently on long-term disability *For inquiries or questions contact: Jennifer White sjwhite8099@ sbcglobal.net*

ACKNOWLEDGEMENTS

A portion of proceeds generated from this book will be donated to the American Cancer Society. The book is a memorial to my mother Bettye M. White and father Robert (Bob) White who fought an admirable battle against a formidable disease and raised three grateful children This book is dedicated to my mother who instilled in me a passion to write, love of literature, and the desire to stand up for my beliefs. To my father whose quiet, yet powerful commitment to the truth helped me develop compassion and honesty. To my husband Steve, my touchstone for 26 years. Thank you Steve for helping me get through the hardest part of my life. To my sister Darla who has helped me remember what is important in life and brother Keith a passionate and talented surgeon who has seen much more death in his life than he should have had to. I am particularly satisfied to have this book completed. With severe brain damage, it is a work of passion. I quit writing this book several times after mixing up the chronology of subject matter, correcting a number of mispellings, using incorrect references and just being too dog tired to write. I also wrote a large portion of this book with one eye closed. Since I had a brain stem stroke it affected my once perfect vision. I am glad I did not quit. I would also like to acknowledge my family on my husband's side. I appreciate all of you. You have taught me things unknown to you and raised a son who is honest, good, and compassionate. I am lucky to have him in my life.

CHAPTER 1

THE HISTORY OF LOUISIANA

The history of Louisiana can be tracked back thousands of years. The "Pelican State" (LA's nickname and state bird) was admitted to the Union as the 18th state in 1812 and is famous for gumbo, shrimp etouffee, beignets, jambalaya, alligators, Mardi Gras, Cajun and Creole culture and much more. Louisiana was named for King Louis XIV and has a rich history that is heavily influenced by the French culture. The city of Dempsey, Louisiana, where this book is set, is most notable for its neighbor on the southeast region of Louisiana...a cultural gem of a city popular for its annual Mardi Gras festivities and a colorful and diverse population. The city is well-known for its superior jazz and blues music and has produced a number of national talents who have ultimately become superstars. The city has employed and educated many Dempsey residents who share a cultural symbiosis relationship with the Big Easy. The two cities, both on the banks of the Mississippi River transports tons of products through the portal of the river everyday. The 5th largest city on the Mississippi, Dempsey has helped facilitate almost 500 million tons of freight that is transported on the river each year. Dempsey is the capital of Louisiana and houses a Historic State

Capital, a flagship University and some of the most diverse populations in the country. Dempsey is known for jazz, blues and zydeco music similar to its close neighbor "The Big Easy" that is located about 60 miles away in the south-eastern part of the state. Both cities are also known for their delicious Creole and Cajun foods and laid back "laissez le bon temps rouler (let the good times roll)" attitude. Dempsey is located about an hour away from the Mardi Gras city, and has a kick-ass college football team that houses a number of fun loving and super cool students. Many of the students who attend Dempsey University are from other states and come to school in Dempsey to get their party legs stretched out. Dempsey is a college town surrounded by fern bars and daiquiri shops and has hosted many national conferences from around the country. The city is chocked full of taco and burrito restaurants, and college memorabilia stores. Dempsey is located in a state that honors the culture with its crawfish, boudin, jambalaya, strawberries, catfish, French food, and Natchitoches Christmas Festival. Both Dempsey and the Mardi Gras city are very hot and enjoy a luscious landscape due to high humidity and subtropical climates. Both cities are hot and sticky, and you could break a sweat by simply walking a short distance. Gardens in both locations produce beautiful landscapes known for their excellent flowers, trees and shrubs. In fact, the southern state mentioned here was heralded as nature's environmental beauty and the envy of many states. Cool temperatures in Dempsey are short-lived and there are only about two months out of the year that can be classified as the cool season. Frequently you could still hear air conditioners whirling past fall. During this time of the year you saw the "shedders". The shedders were residents who tried to be stylish with winter clothing too early and became hot and started shedding their clothing early in the year. Then, you had the "burners". These were the residents of either city who refused to shed their hot clothing even when they were burning up. You could identify the "burners" from their soaked and sweaty clothing. Their motto was "It's better to look good than to feel good." If you were close enough, you could hear the loud rumble of the college football games in Dempsey on Saturday night pulsate with the vibrations from the crowd's excitement. There was nothing like it. Approximately 80,000+ people cheering and yelling for the football team to win...win...win! Everything else was forgotten for one night. Everyone who attended the Saturday night football games had something in common. The love of winning. Or...the compassion of losing. People attending the game would arrive early to get a good seat if they didn't have season tickets which most people owned. The sororities and fraternities had their own section where they sat during the football games. Prior to the football game, the greeks would respectfully cheer on their team... until the drinks started to flow. As the football game proceeded, the intoxicated greeks who had consumed a number of drinks would become animated, vulgar and aggressive. But, that was okay because everyone loved Saturday night football! You would see little girls with cheerleader outfits on and little boys with football outfits on running around and dancing to music in their heads before the band started to play. College football games were a legacy for the people of Dempsey...a tradition...a namesake. Most Louisiana families owned yard signs, beer mugs, and clothing that promoted their college football team. Nothing like that Cajun spirit!

CHAPTER 2

THE CONOVERS

Harry Sr. Conovers was the son of Eubert and Ella Conovers. He was a rich man who made his living growing vegetables and raising cattle in Dallas. His mother and father were of Dutch/Flemish descent and were well-respected in the Dallas, TX agriculture community. The Conovers family were well-known in the Dallas area for farming and ranching proficiency. They made millions of dollars in the farming business and associated with an extremely well-off group of farmers. Although his mother and father were well-respected within the Highland Park community where they lived, their only son Harry Sr. Conovers was considered a bad seed to the people in Dallas and unfortunately to his own parents. As a child, he often verbally assaulted his parents and physically hit his mom. As he grew up in the Dallas area, he was a bully at his school and a regular visitor to the principal's office. Although his parents blamed his bad behavior on the fact that "he was young", Harry Sr. never emerged from his mean ways. As a teen, his mother and father enrolled him in behavior modification classes. He would run away from the classes. After a series of stealing incidents, Eubert took a belt to the boy and lost his temper as he beat his son to a pulp. Although Eubert's Dutch background taught him to never beat a child, he lost his temper. Eubert then prayed nonstop for hours to seek forgiveness for the beating. Harry Sr. never got over the beating he got from his father and carried his anger over into his adulthood. The incident caused Harry Sr. and his father to emotionally split. The two had never been close so nothing really changed between the dad and son. Although the father and son were never close and rarely saw eye to eye, Harry Sr. learned the craft of farming and ranching from his father. He learned how to select the best crops to grow and the profitable cattle to buy. Although his father taught him everything he learned about the farming business, Harry Sr. never gave him any credit for the knowledge. He thought his father was too meek and weak and lacked masculinity. However, the Conovers owned a large estate on 1,000 acres and were very successful at farming. They grew barley, wheat, corn, soybeans and eventually tobacco. They also bought a number of livestock animals (sheep, goats, cows and chickens) that they would use to market milk, eggs, wool and meat for humans. One day his father asked Harry Sr. to drive to a suburb of Dallas to buy a list of farm supplies needed to spray his fields and add vitamins to the soil.

CHAPTER 3

MEETING BELLE

Harry Sr. had trouble finding the product in Dallas but knew he could get it in a Dallas suburb called Youngsport. The city was about 40 minutes away so Harry Sr. hemmed and hawed about the drive. Unfortunately, the closer hardware store to his home did not have the items he needed for his father. So Harry Sr. decided to drive a little further to find the items. As he entered the city of Youngsport, TX, Harry Sr. saw a sign indicating there was a hardware store there. During his unscheduled trip to Youngsport, Harry Sr. bumped into a young girl on main street named Belle McFadden. Belle was dressed in wide-leg pants with a pretty button-down puffy sleeve shirt. She was average in size and had a pretty face. Harry Sr. took to Belle quickly. He asked her a question that he already knew the answer, but the question generated a response from Belle and ignited a conversation between the two. Harry asked Belle where the hardware store was. Belle pointed to the store directly in front of the two. Slightly embarrassed by his obvious cluelessness, Harry Sr. promptly walked into the store. Belle followed as she needed to buy something for her father's phonograph that he was renovating. Although Harry really needed a gardening store, he acted as if he needed a tool from the hardware store so he could continue his chat with Belle. So as he was acting like he was looking for something, Harry saw Belle and said "funny seeing you again". Then, he privately rolled his eyes at himself noticing how cheesy the comment sounded. Belle responded to the comment with a giggle and said "yes, funny". After a few more pleasantries, Harry Sr. said he had to get going and asked Belle for her phone number. After leaving the hardware store, Harry Sr. stopped by a garden store and bought the soil vitamins his father needed. He then left for home. Since Belle lived in Youngsport, she was home some time before Harry Sr. who had about a 40 minute trip ahead of him. During his trip home, Harry Sr. felt a euphoria that he did not quite recognize…the euphoria was named Belle McFadden. At around 7:00 pm Harry Sr. called Belle and asked her to dinner on Friday night. She said "yes, of course" and was excited about seeing Harry Sr. again. On Friday, Harry Sr. picked Belle up from Youngsport at 7:00. As he remembered when he met her, she was nicely dressed and prompt which Harry Sr. liked very much. They had dinner at a steak restaurant in Youngsport, and Harry Sr. was surprised at Belle's healthy appetite. "Boy you really put that steak up didn't you?" Harry said not aware that eating was a sensitive subject to Belle whose parents would always tease her about food and tell her she could lose a few pounds. After Belle explained to Harry Sr. why his comment was insensitive, Harry Sr. apologized, and the conversation moved forward. "Well Belle, what kind of things do you like to do?" Harry asked. Belle said, "Well, I like to grow food in our garden. My family has a Victory Garden* in our yard." *Victory Gardens were planted during WWI and II as a way to deal with food shortages during the war. The crops grown helped feed the soldiers and helped families during food and other supply rationings. Harry reciprocated "That's interesting Belle. What kind of food do you grow?" Harry Sr. asked Belle. She responded "Potatoes, peas and stuff like that. My family also cans its own vegetables." Harry Sr. responded "Wow, you guys do it all." After Harry Sr.'s conversation with Belle, he had second thoughts about taking Belle out on a date. He told his parents, "I think she is poor. They only eat things they pick from the ground!" Harry Sr.'s mother said "Oh, THOSE kind of people. They probably have a Victory Garden too!" she continued. Harry Sr. responded "They do!" The negative comment by Harry Sr.'s mom did not deter Harry's interest in Belle. He continued to see Belle for several more months. Although Harry Sr. wasn't in love with Belle, he wanted to get out of his house. So, he proposed. He asked Belle for her hand in marriage in the least romantic way. He and Belle were on a tractor brush hogging some of his parent's land. Harry Sr. basically screamed his proposal to Belle who had to ask him twice what he said. Then he screamed "Want to get married!" Belle finally heard Harry Sr. and was excited to be asked to get married. She said "Yes, of course." Harry Sr. said "Okay then. We'll get married at the Justice of the Peace next Tuesday." was a little disappointed that she would not have a church wedding but, she was still excited that she would be married. Belle dated very little and never thought she would marry. She was flattered that she had been asked. On Tuesday, Harry Sr. woke up, put on his best suit and drove to Youngsport to marry Belle McFadden. They would marry at the local courthouse, take no honeymoon, and eat lunch at the local diner. He had chicken fried steak and Belle had chicken and dumplings. They each ordered a piece of pie as a celebratory gesture and then left the restaurant. The frugal celebration that occurred on Belle and Harry Sr.'s wedding day was not from lack of funds but lack of interest on Harry Sr.'s part. After getting married in Youngsport, Texas, Belle and Harry Sr. Conovers bought a house in the Dallas community next to his parents. The couple subsequently had a child named Harry Jr. who became the boil on the ass of the residents in the Dallas community where they lived. Harry Jr. was a premature child and never learned the importance of hard work or integrity. During his childhood in the Dallas area, Jr. was sent to the most prestigious school, wore the most expensive clothes and owned the newest gadgets on the market. His parents did not know what to do with Harry Jr. other than to buy him things. So, they did. Neither Belle nor Harry Sr. were capable of showing Jr. parental love and support. And, as the year's progressed, Harry Jr. carried on the parental drought of never showing his family love. In Dallas, Harry Sr. and Belle Conovers developed their "farm legs" with money from Harry Sr.'s parent's death. With the money, he bought land and farm animals he needed to start his own farm in Dallas. As he continued to build his farm, Harry Sr. bought more land and more cattle. A few years later, Harry Sr. was a gazillionaire. Harry Sr. had developed a real knack for growing profitable crops and raising cattle. But, he was a strange man...sadly haunted by the obsession to make money and own things. Belle, Harry Sr.'s wife, was a pleasant enough woman but could not work her way through some of the dark memories of her past. And, she was persistently depressed by the infidelity that Harry Sr. brought into her life and the terrible relationship she had with her own family. Also, the Conovers were not particularly well liked in their Dallas community. The Conovers were greedy and shallow. And, Jr., the son proved to be a little brat who learned to love money from his parents and be-came obsessed with what Belle and Harry Sr. would leave him after they died. Harry Sr. frequently compared himself to Jr. as money was concerned. He would always tell Belle, "That boy loves money as much as I do. I would always wonder what my parents would leave me when they were gone. But, after we had that argument a few years ago about something I can't remember for the life of me, they may not give me diddly squat!" Harry Jr. would tell Belle that he was mad as hell at his mother and father but could not for the life of him-self remember why. Harry Jr. wondered why his father never saw his relatives. But, every time he asked why, his father would lash out and have "one of his episodes" as he called it. Harry Sr. regularly claimed he was going to have an episode so Belle and Harry Jr. knew to drop the subject and move back from the father's space. All Belle would say is "naturally". Luckily, it turned out okay for Harry Sr.. After his parents died, they left him quite a significant inheritance and lots of acreage. Although Harry Sr. was given the money he needed to start his farming business, he was quite adept at making financial deals with the townspeople in Texas. He was never willing to acknowledge the good-luck and wealth that he had acquired from his parents, Harry Sr. cursed them until his death. Again, he couldn't remember why he hated them…he just hated them. Harry Jr. attended middle and high school in the Dallas area before moving to Dempsey where he graduated from high school. As he was raised, his family obtained a significant amount of wealth from selling acres of crops he raised and the cattle he sold. Over the years, Harry Sr.'s farm got bigger and bigger and so did his pocketbook. Planting crops and raising tasty beef was a generational norm in the Conovers' family. Harry Jr. would continue the tradition as he grew up in Dempsey, LA. After the wedding, Belle moved to Dallas with Harry Sr. into his mother and father's extra bedroom. Harry Sr.'s parents were never fond of Belle. Both thought she was not from the "right" family based on Conovers' stock. Prior to their marriage, Harry Sr. tried, unsuccessfully, to sell Belle to his mother and father. He would tell them what a good cook she was and how well she kept the house, but his parents never seemed to catch on to the endorsement and never warmed up to Belle. Harry Sr. was hoping for a substantial wedding gift from his parents. But, his parents decided to buy he and Belle a traditional wedding gift of everyday dishes. Harry Sr. never forgave his parents for the "lame" wedding gift as he called it. He told Belle, "They have so much damn money that they will never run out. And they give us a crappy set of dishes for our wedding. They are just greedy!" Harry Sr. said. Belle commented, "Well I think the dishes are very nice, and they look expensive. We will use them often." Harry replied "you would say they are nice…you always say everything is nice!" Harry Sr.'s face turned blood red and he yelled "Dishes/fishes Belle! We can't live in a dish. I'm going to have to get an expensive mortgage and pray that my salary from the farm helps us out.!" As Harry Sr. and Belle drove to his parent's house where they would stay until they bought a house of their own, Harry Sr. bitched about having a new mortgage the entire way to his parent's house. "My parents are sooo lame. They have more money than they know what to do with and they waste it on useless items." Belle said, "Well Harry Sr. it is their money." He replied, "no, it is my money!" This day marked the exact moment that Belle recognized a flaw in Harry Sr.'s personality. There would be many more to come throughout their marriage. Although Harry Sr. worked with his dad in their farming business and made plenty of money, but he resented having to pay for a house. Harry Sr. was extremely frugal or as Belle called him "cheap." The couple were married at Harry Sr.'s mother and father's house and Harry Sr.'s father gave him a bill for a large part of the ceremony. Harry Sr. asked Belle "have you ever seen anything like this? Don't you think it is odd that my parents expect me to reimburse thfor our wedding?" He thought his parents should have picked up the bill for the wedding and a new place to live for he and Belle.

CHAPTER 4

BELLE'S PREGNANT

It was barely a month after Belle and Harry Sr. were married when she became pregnant with her first and only child. Belle said to Harry Sr. "If the baby is a boy, I want to call him Harry Jr. like his father. If the baby is a girl, I would like to call her Harriett. Harry responded, "Well I hope it is a boy". I don't care about what we call the baby Belle." After Belle and Harry's marriage, and the delivery of their first child, Harry Sr. purchased a new home that was located directly by his mother and father. The house that Harry Sr. purchased for he, Belle and the new baby was small but sufficient for two adults and a child. The house had two bedrooms, 1 1/2 baths and a fenced yard for a dog that they would never have. Belle's pregnancy was fairly normal although her tremendous weight gain (45 lbs) caused high blood pressure and an added amount of concern for her Obstetrician (OB). Belle had done nothing to help herself with her weight gain. Every office appointment that she had included a 30-minute lecture from her OB about pregnancy and weight gain and a 20-minute trip to a local fast-food restaurant. "I deserve it!" Belle would say. The OB's lecture rolled off Belle's back as she ordered her normal triple cheeseburger with large fries after every OB appointment. During the drive home from her OB appointment, she would scarf down the fast food and collect a pile of crumbs in her lap and the passenger seat of her car. Although Harry Sr. rarely paid attention to Belle, he noticed her weight gain and the crumbs she left on her face and shirt from the food she ate on the drive home. Harry Sr. would make mean comments to Belle about eating on the way home from her OB. Masquerading as concern, Harry Sr. would scold Belle for eating so much and used the newborn as a reason he was concerned. Harry would say Belle "why areyou polluting yourself and our child with all of that fast food when you are pregnant." Then, Belle would cry, and Harry Sr. would apologize…and life went on. Belle experienced terrible morning sickness and lower back pain. Harry Sr. in his horrible Harry Sr. way would try to make Belle laugh when she was in obvious pain. She would tell Harry to just be nice when I feel bad. He would say "I can't. I don't know how." This day marked the exact moment that Belle recognized a second flaw in Harry Sr.'s personality. On a stormy Friday, the 13th in a Dallas, TX hospital maternity ward Harry Conovers Jr. was born. Although he had asthma that sounded like a box of rocks rattling through his 7 lb. frame, his delivery was normal. Belle was fine but her blood pressure had spiked during the delivery. After the delivery she said, "Well, I guess I had too many cheeseburgers when I was pregnant." Harry Sr. rolled his eyes and said "You think!" Harry Jr. came out screaming like a cat on fire. Belle chose not to breast feed, and she had difficulty getting Harry Jr. to take a bottle. After what seemed to be forever, the baby finally grabbed the nipple of the bottle and gulped down the milk. "Look at him suck that milk Harry Sr. This boy is hungry!" Harry Sr. said, "I hope he turns out to be a strong and active boy when he grows up so he can help me on the farm!" Belle said "He is going to be my big boy who is gonna help out in the house!" At this point Harry Sr. shot Belle a mean look and took her comment as a personal cut to him. When Belle was pregnant, mothers stayed in the hospital for up to 10 days after giving birth.

She could not smoke until Harry Jr. was taken to the nursery. Then she quickly lit-up. Harry Sr. despised Belle's smoking habit. He thought her to be careless and lack discipline. Belle did not care. She was 100% addicted to cigarettes.

CHAPTER 5

WHERE IS HARRY JR.?

Harry Jr. was released from the hospital on day 7. Belle was getting her things ready to leave the hospital and she realized that Harry Sr. was not to be found. She asked the nurse...she asked a hospital attendant...but there was no Harry Sr. What Belle did not know is that during the time when she was inquiring about Harry Sr., he was chatting with a nurse in the hallway. The nurse was an attractive blond hair thin built 25 year-old who was unmarried and interested in Harry Sr. The nurse, whose name was Barbara, lived in Dallas with her 10-year-old poodle named Bomber. She and Harry Sr. were not at all discreet with their flirtations. Before Harry Sr. left the hospital, Barbara passed him her phone number on a little sheet of paper with her personal artwork...a heart, arrow, and a set of lips she created with her lipstick. Belle knew nothing of Harry Sr.'s encounter with the nurse. His affair started on the day he left the hospital from Harry Jr.'s birth. As he entered the hospital room where Belle was staying, Harry Sr. was overly attentive to Belle because he felt guilty about flirting with the nurse. When he finally went back into Belle's room she said, "Where have you been Harry. It seems to have been hours since I saw you last." Harry replied "No it hasn't been that long. I got lost walking the halls trying to find this room." Belle then said "Well, we have been released. Jr. is in the nursery. We can pick him up and head home." Harry Sr. said "Oh, good. Boy am I ready." After Belle and Harry Sr. picked up Jr. from the nursery, Belle was escorted to a wheelchair that would assist her in exiting the hospital. Harry Sr. signed some papers, and the family walked to the exit of the hospital where he had parked his truck. The ride to Harry Sr. and Belle's new home was not calm. Harry Jr. was screaming like a sick animal and Belle was stressed to the hilt. Harry Sr. was calm and surprisingly pleasant since he just chatted with his new girlfriend. Upon arriving at their house, Belle and Harry Sr. unloaded the car, took Harry Jr. inside and laid him down on the bed in the second bedroom of the house. For several weeks Belle spent her time taking care of a newborn who wasn't crazy about taking a bottle, slept only a few hours each night and cried most of the day and night. What did Harry Sr. do? Not much actually. He refused to change diapers, feed the baby and complained all the time about not getting any sleep. Harry Sr. stayed outside most of the day tending to his crops that were recently planted and fed his animals. But, every day he ran into town…specifically to the hospital where Jr. was born to see Barbara the nurse he met when Jr. was born. The couple had a routine. Harry Sr. would pick Barbara up on her lunch hour, they would have some kissy-face in his truck that eventually led to sex in the truck, eat a little lunch and then say good-by until the next day. Then each of them would return to their jobs and not talk until the next day. Belle knew nothing about Harry's affair with the nurse. She became a little suspicious when the phone would ring several times and no one responded to her "hello". But, Belle was really not the suspicious type and was too preoccupied with her baby to care. Had she known about Harry Sr.'s affair, she probably would be secretly happy that Harry Sr. was getting it somewhere. During Jr.'s birth Belle had an episiotomy (surgical incision made at the opening of the vagina to aid in childbirth to prevent tissue rupture) that was extremely painful. In addition to the episiotomy, she was having major post partem depression. For someone like Belle who already suffered from depression, post-partum virtually felt the same as everyday of her life. After a few months of romps in the truck, sex in the seat and sloppy kissy face, Barbara took a job in another city and moved from Dallas to Oklahoma where her father was dealing with a terminal illness. After attempting to keep the affair alive between Barbara and Harry Sr., the long distance relationship proved too difficult for the couple. Harry Sr. did not have the patience for a long-distance affair, and Barbara was bored with Harry Sr. anyway. Unfortunately Harry Sr. and Barbara's affair did not mark the end of Harry's infidelity. He was a serial cheater and would continue to have affairs his entire marriage. Immediately after Barbara left Dallas, Harry Sr. started seeing a woman from his church who was recently divorced. Although Belle did not know that Harry Sr. was taken with Ellen, a woman from her adult Sunday school class, she was curious as to why Harry Sr. became motivated to attend Sunday school and church. Immediately after Sunday school, Ellen and Harry would meet up in the back of the baptismal pool area of the church. They fooled around where the new Christians changed their clothes for baptism. Although there were a lot of references to God during their love making, the references were not Christian-like at all. Rumors did fly among the adult Sunday School class regarding Ellen and Harry Sr.'s relationship. But, the rumors seemed to excite the couple rather than make them feel guilty about screwing around on Harry Sr.'s wife and Ellen's boyfriend. When living in Dallas, Harry Sr. purchased a lot of land to grow grain, sorghum, rice, corn, wheat, tobacco, and corn. In Harry Sr.'s mind, Harry Jr. would grow up helping him raise cattle and grow crops. Unfortunately, this was Harry Sr.'s dream...for his son to apprentice with him on the farm. But, Harry Jr. had other plans. He was not interested in apprenticing with his father on the farm. Harry Jr.'s interest in farming was dismal and fleeting. Instead of working with his father on the farm, he would run from the animals that his father asked him to feed. And, Jr. would scream when the animals approached him. And, he would complain about the plants being dirty and smelly. He had asthma that required Albuterol for his condition, and he was as skinny as a stick with very little strength or stamina. Harry Sr. and Belle did not need two incomes so Belle was a stay-at-home mother and raised Harry Jr. basically on her own. Harry Sr. pretty much ignored the boy and kept seeing Ellen from his church. Belle started to get suspicious of Harry Sr. when she would try and find Harry Sr. at church and he would be in the the back of the baptismal area. One time this happened, Belle asked Harry "what on earth are you doing here?" Harry Sr. was tucking in his shirt and said "Oh, I was looking for the bathroom." Belle said, "Well tuck in your shirt, and I'll show you where it is." Harry Sr. took a deep breath and was happy that this was not the day that Ellen would meet Belle. As Harry Sr. was working his land in Dallas, he hired several fieldhands to help him plant and work on the farm. Although Harry Jr. was a young boy, he liked to piddle and help his father on the farm where he could. He started helping his father with rudimentary tasks, and as he grew up, his father started relying on him to complete harder duties. But, Harry Jr.'s growing up seemed to do nothing for his interest in farming. His father noticed that he was slow at learning new tasks and lacked patience. He hated to admit it, but Harry Sr. told Belle that Harry Jr. just didn't have it. She asked "have what". Harry Sr. said "the boy doesn't have the fire in his belly to get things done. I am afraid that he is not going to be helpful to me. He'll cause me more work." Belle was frustrated and said "Well Harry Sr. you are not always in control." And that was the last thing in addition to a few larger annoyances that Belle recognized as being a real problem with Harry Sr.

CHAPTER 6

FAILED EXPECTATIONS

O ver the years Jr. never developed a passion for farming as Harry Sr. would have liked. Jr. did not like to get his hands or his clothes dirty that was unavoidable on the farm. Belle did not like to hear Harry Sr. talk negatively about Jr. She would tell Harry Sr. "if you don't have anything nice to say about your son, don't say anything!" Harry Sr. responded "You have to be frickin kidding me Belle. I am not your child! I think you have forgotten that. So, shut it and mind your own business!" Belle in her submissive voice responded "okay." Basically, Belle agreed with Harry Sr. for the most part about Jr. But, as a mother, she was too embarrassed to admit it. She thought in addition to his laziness, negativity, and self-ishness, he was a little effeminate and weak. Although both of Jr.'s parents were not very proud of Jr., they talked him up to their friends at church and the community as being a smart and caring boy. However, to anyone who listened to Harry Sr.'s gibberish about Jr. being strong and smart they would laugh behind his back. The truth was that Harry Jr. was frail and could barely walk a few steps without breathing hard and sucking on his Albuterol cartridge. He was not necessarily weak from any injury or sickness but had no interest in trying anything new. Harry Jr. was also very dramatic and a major complainer so a lot of people would call him "hapless Harry". Harry

Jr.'s apparent weakness angered the fieldhands who worked at Harry Sr.'s Dallas farm. They did not believe that Harry Sr. or Harry Jr. carried the awesome weight of the farm that they were expected to carry. When Harry Sr. would hear them complain about Harry Jr., Harry Sr. would yell at them and say "my son is not required to carry the weight that the fieldhands are expected. He is my son, and this farm is MINE! So, shut it and get back to work now!" And that is the way it was with Harry Sr. He never showed his fieldhands any compassion and was extremely hard on all of them. When a female fieldhand would ask for a couple of hours off to take her child to the doctor, she had to go through a major inquisition by Harry Sr. He would ask questions like "What is wrong with the child?. And say "Can't you take her/him to the doctor on days you don't have to work? There are doctors who work on the weekend. Have you asked about this option?" Harry Sr. always required a doctor's excuse from any of the staff who asked for time off for a doctor's appointment. The situation that Harry Sr. created at his farm was hostile and unfriendly. He acted like a dictator and was cruel, and the field hands where bullied by Harry Sr. He would always tell Belle that "I like to be feared by my employees, not respected!" He was definitely feared by his employees, and most of them did not like he or Jr. Although Belle was liked more so than the Harry's, she was not liked that much either by the fieldhands. Harry Sr.'s staff thought that his son Harry Jr. was a spoiled brat. When Harry Sr. did not get the respect he felt that he deserved, he would slap the employees and dock their pay. He was sued a dozen times for being such a jerk and physically abusive, but the complaints never stuck because he knew people that could make the complaints disappear. Harry Sr. often beat his employees and sent a few to the hospital for their injuries. One employee was beaten with a farm implement used to bale hay. Another was hit in the face with a rock and the employee's eye was bloodied. One employee told another that if Harry Sr. wanted respect, he needed to

show the employees respect. Those words proved worthless and
without any retribution. Harry Sr. would tell his Texas friend Jackson
"Those N's (he did not use the initial) should be glad they have a job.
I have to explain things a couple of times to them so they understand
what I am saying. Most of them are dumb as dirt!" Not the sharpest
tools in the shed. If you know what I mean. I gave them a job...no
one else did...and I think they owe me. I risked my reputation by
hiring these people. You know how the town folk feel about the
blackies. I saved them from going hungry. Without me...their families would starve!" Harry Sr. carried on in his racist rhetoric repeat-
ing incorrect stereotypes about the African American culture.
Jackson, whose best friend was an African American man, endured
Harry Sr.'s racist rants as long as he could stand them. Jackson knew
how obnoxious Harry Sr. could be about his employees, and he was
appalled at Harry Sr.'s continued archaic views of the African
American community. Jackson's best-friend, Al, was an African
American man and a regular guest in Jackson's house. Jackson's
family had known Al and his family for years, and he loved his children. So, hearing negative comments regularly about the African
American people weighed heavily on Jackson. On this day Jackson
had had it with Harry Sr.. He told him (Harry Sr.) that he was an
imbecile and knew nothing about the African American people.
Harry Sr. was shaken and told Jackson that he did not mean any
harm. At that point, Jackson raised a fist to Harry Sr. and screamed
"you never do!". Jackson then left Harry Sr. forever. On his way
home, Jackson smiled and gave a quick "alright" yell. He was proud
of himself for finally sticking up to a man who proved to have bad
values. When Jackson finally reached his home, he opened the door
to his house, saw his wife and children gathered in the television
room and smiled. He was happy. Jackson told his wife that he was
no longer friends with Harry Sr. who was a bigot and bad man. His
wife, Kate, was happy and told Jackson that she had never liked

Harry Sr.. She said "he has always disgust me. You know that he never looked me in the eye?" Jackson responded "I can't believe that it took me this long to see the real Harry Conovers Sr. He was shady and a know it all, and I never want to see that damn racist again!" Jackson finished. Kate continued, "He was gross and smacked his food. He never thanked me for any meal I cooked for him, as if he expected it! I never said anything to you because I thought you liked him." Jackson said "I did like him until he started talking negatively about African Americans, talked incessantly about how he fooled around on Belle and became such a know it all." Jackson then hugged Katie and apologized to her for bringing Harry Sr. around their family. Then, Jackson's family gathered around the dinner table, held hands and thanked the Lord for their family. Belle Conovers was kind to the employees, and they liked her. Of course, she maintained her ice-cold demeanor around Harry Sr. and talked ill about the employees to him, but to their face, she was kind. Occasionally, she would bring the fieldhands cookies and a cold glass of water in a paper cup only. Harry Sr. could care less if one of his fieldhands had a heat stroke. Harry Sr. did not like Belle being nice to the field staff. He would tell her not to be nice to the "hands." Belle would say "I don't want our staff to hate me Harry. They work hard and I would rather them like me than not. You don't get that. I get it. Don't expect me to be unkind because you are!!" Harry Sr. did not expect the outburst he received from Belle. He stammered and said "Okay then! Didn't mean to get you in a tizzy!' Belle just rolled her eyes. The next day, she made cookies and gave them to the staff. Belle expected the response she would get from Harry Sr. She would give the cookies out to the staff and Harry Sr. would say to Belle "You need to watch yourself around the fieldhands. They view kindness as weakness and that could get out of hand. Don't want to see you get hurt." She would laugh at Harry and tell him "Funny you are afraid your employees will hurt me. It is sad, but they are nicer to me than you are

Harry." The insult rolled off the back of Harry Conovers. He had a pattern of not listening to Belle. And, over the years, Harry Conovers Sr. had become an insensitive, mean man who lost the love of a good woman and the admiration of a son. Belle told Harry Sr. "If you were nicer to your fieldhands they would be nicer to you. He then replied "Not gonna happen!" Harry failed to understand why his staff hated him. Nor did he understand why his wife resented him and his son thought he was a joke. One time, one of the employees looked at Belle a little too long in Harry Sr.'s opinion. Harry Sr. told the man that he "better look the other way or he would do what they did in the 50's to those people." Harry Sr. was referring to the incident in 1955 when the 14-year-old Emmett Till was abducted, tortured and lynched for flirting with a white 21-year-old woman in a Mississippi grocery store. The young man looked confused. He was not even born in the fifty's and had only learned of the racial tension sur-rounding the Emmett Till story from history class. This was simply another example of Harry Sr. being out of touch with reality. The field staff did not feel like lynching was out of the question if Harry Sr. was mad enough….and, Harry Sr. was always mad. Although the employees were scared of Harry Sr., the workers would blast Harry Sr, when he wasn't around, they would make jokes about him. One employee named George made everyone laugh when he mocked Harry Sr. He would say "Yea mista Conovers. I sure do get what ya talkin bout. Don't beat me sir, please sir don't beat me!" George's friends would laugh until they cried at the man who made fun of Harry Sr.. George would also talk about Harry Jr.. He would say "that boy is a bad seed…mean to the core. His father outta take him to the woods by the field and beat the shit out of that little bastard!" Again, the field hands roared with laughter as George filled his lower lip with tobacco. Because the field hands hated Harry Jr., they decided as a group that they would treat him like a girl. One of the female field staff exclaimed "Yea, we'll call him Bernadette instead of Harry.

And, we'll give him, I mean her, a little pink outfit that we can buy for practically nothing at the dollar store. Then, we'll give Harry, I mean Bernadette, a couple of bucks to wear the clothes around town. It will be a hoot!" Everyone of the field hands agreed to the plan. But then one day, Harry Jr. had one of the hot pink sundresses on and he ran into his father. Stacy, one of the fieldhands had offered Harry Jr. five dollars to carry a purse. So, as he was wearing a hot pink sundress and carrying a purse, Harry Jr. bumped into his father who screamed. "Harry Jr. what in the hell do you have on? You are going to be the laughing stock of Dallas and embarrass your parents!" Harry Jr. replied "Stacy said that I would look good, and so I did it. She gave me a few dollars." Harry Sr. screamed at Harry Jr. and said "Boy, go change your clothes. I will deal with Stacy!" Harry Jr. was infatuated with money so he would do practically anything for a buck. He would get a five dollar bill for telling his father to "F" off another five to kiss one of the male farmhands. He told the staff that he had no pride when it came to money. Harry Jr. became obsessed with money. Harry Sr. quizzed the staff on who was responsible for Harry's "ridiculous appearance". No one fessed up so Harry Sr. beat all of them. He did not necessarily care that Harry Jr. looked like a fool. He cared mostly about his reputation tanking from Harry Jr.'s antics. When Harry Sr. beat his employees, he lost his temper. He left marks on the employees' legs and buttocks. The employees had 0 respect for the Conovers. They referred to the family as the three B's...Harry Sr...the bigot, Harry Jr. the brat and Belle...the bitch wife with an extra note that she could be nice.. Harry Jr. disliked his father's obvious snobbery when it came to people who were not like him...who did not have his same opinions...who dressed differently, etc.. But, Harry Jr. knew that it was an unwinnable battle to try to get his father to think differently. And, his opinions were similar to his father's anyway.

CHAPTER 7

THE ODD FAMILY

The Conovers' family was quite odd. They were all short and each had their own monogrammed stepping tool to help them reach things. If one of them used the incorrect stepping stool all hell broke loose in the Conovers household. The family was selfish and shared with no one. Each family member had their favorite ice cream container emblazoned with their names on the carton. If one of the Conovers ate the other Conover's ice cream all hell would break loose in the Conover's household. Harry Sr.'s parents had personally earned their wealth through farming and then passed on the wealth to Harry Sr. It was from his parent's work that he had accumulated a lot of wealth. It was not contributable to Harry Sr.'s efforts. Although he made money selling crops and raising cattle, Harry Sr. misled many people when he told them he had worked his fingers to the bone to acquire all he had. It was an untruth that would follow him until the day he died. Harry Sr.'s contorted view of his personal wealth was handed down to Harry Jr. who believed that his father had worked for his wealth. Harry Jr. referred to his family's wealth at the most inappropriate times as he grew up in Dallas and then eventually in Dempsey. He also bragged often about his parent's money and the businesses they owned. When at school, Harry Jr. would brag to his friends and teachers about his parent's wealth. As the years passed, the Conovers became known as the greedy rich family to everyone who knew them. Harry Jr. attended school in Dallas for years, but he was not active in school activities. He kept to himself...in his little weird world. For years Belle and Harry Sr. tried to get Harry Jr. interested in some kind of art or sporting activity. All Harry Jr. wanted to do was lay around, watch television, and play video games. One time in Dallas, Jr. invited a friend from his school to come by his house to play video games. Belle and Harry Sr. hoped that the relationship between Harry Jr. and the visiting friend would work out for their son. Then suddenly a fight broke out between the boy and Jr., and the parent's hopes were gone. The boy who was visiting Jr. claimed that Jr. was cheating, and he was. After punching Jr., the boy left angry. That was the last friend Jr. ever asked to his house. Belle and Harry Sr. were very disappointed and never encouraged Jr. to ask anyone over again. While at school in Dallas, Harry Jr. was stand-offish and maintained an air of superiorship among the teachers and students. The school's general opinion of Harry Jr. was not positive. The students at Harry Jr.'s school thought the boy was a know-it-all and arrogant. The teachers ignored Jr. and spoke negatively about him in the teacher's lounge. As for the Conovers' family, they were not well-liked in the Dallas community where they lived. Belle and Harry Sr. would ingratiate themselves with people who had a lot of money but failed to establish any real friendships with anyone in Dallas. After spending several years in Texas and making a fortune in the farming industry, Harry Sr. decided it was time to move to broader pastures. His friend Patrick and his wife Susan lived in a city in Louisiana called Dempsey. Most of the farming and cattle publications that Patrick read mentioned a southern farming area that was highly productive. The city was called Dempsey. Patrick and Susan had made a significant amount of money in Dempsey and mentioned the profitable area to Harry Sr.. The word "profitable" made Harry Sr. interested in the area. Patrick shared the news with Harry Sr. who was always eager to try new things. After reading more research on the area, Harry Sr. decided that he and his family would move south.

CHAPTER 8

MOVING SOUTH

After Harry Sr. told Harry Jr. and Belle his decision to move to the south for more farming opportunities, Harry Sr. started getting his ducks in a row for the move. One of the first things he did was end the affair he was having with Ellen. In his cavalier and obnoxious way he told Ellen "It was fun while it lasted doll, but I'm heading out to greener pastures." Ellen said "oh, okay, it was fun". There was no love lost…actually no love at all. The affair had run its course and became boring to Ellen and Harry Sr. so no feelings were affected negatively by either party. The second thing that Harry Sr. did prior to moving his family to Dempsey was purchase a house and land in the new city. He decided that in addition to attending school in Dempsey, he would start a farming business and raise cattle. A few weeks later, with the family car and Harry Jr.'s pet goat Festu in tow, the family started their trip to Dempsey, LA. They would drive to Dempsey in Harry Sr.'s large truck, they towed Belle's car behind Festus's trailor. Harry Sr. did not want to take the goat along for the trip to Dempsey, but Jr. pitched a hissy in favor of taking Festus on the trip. The animal was given to Jr. by Harry Sr. as a diversion tactic to keep him engaged while Belle and he were doing other things. After having to stop a few times to walk Festus, Harry Sr. began to regret agreeing to take the goat to

Dempsey. Harry Jr. slept most of the trip so, Harry Sr. had to walk the goat. He said to Belle "I can't believe I have to move that dirty, annoying, fur ball of Jr.'s to Dempsey. He hasn't helped with the goat at all. I feed him, I clean him. He just brushes him occasionally, and he can't even do that correctly. I don't even like that damn goat! As much as Jr. loves that animal, the more I hate him. It pisses me off!" said Harry Sr. Belle replied, "Well Harry, you bought Jr. the goat so whose responsibility should it be?" Harry Sr rolled his eyes at Belle and told her "The goat is Jr.'s so who do you think should be responsible for the animal?" Belle shrugged. Harry Sr.'s truck was more than roomy for their load with a large back cab where Harry Jr. sat (slept) for the entire trip. Harry Sr. felt responsible for taking care of the goat since Harry Jr. would not. So, he felt especially free to sell the goat immediately when he reached Dempsey. He told Belle, "That annoying piece of animal shit is gone as soon as I have time to sell him." Belle reciprocated "You better make sure Jr. knows. He loves that goat. Are you going to go up against a boy who is weaker and a lot younger than you...not to mention your son!" Harry replied "Hell yes, I'll go up against him. He acts like a little entitled brat." Belle just said "nice" to Harry Sr. As they continued to head toward Dempsey, Harry Sr. said "I don't think it has ever been quieter since Jr. has been asleep." Belle responded "No, I think you are right. It is nice." Then, Harry Jr. jumps up and screams that he had a bad dream. After an inauthentic soothing motion, Belle pats Jr. on the head and tells him everything is alright. Jr. explained to his mother and father that something came to him when he was sleeping. He announced to his parents that he should get the largest bedroom in the house since he was a "growing boy". Harry Sr. told him "Yea right. Keep dreaming Jr. You are such an idiot boy." Belle scolded Harry Sr. for the name calling. Belle's comments pissed Harry Sr. off, and he slapped her on the leg. After years of being slapped and emotionally and physically abused by Harry Sr. Belle had developed an inconsistent spine where at times she would slap Harry Sr. back and at other times she would cry. Harry Jr.'s parent's arguments had become a regular event throughout his life. He normally ignored the anger and tuned out their voices and today was no different than every other day with the Conovers. Harry Sr. and Belle would argue and the next second act as if nothing happened. Harry Jr. became used to the behavior of the Conover.

CHAPTER 9

ENTERING DEMPSEY

After a very long drive, the Conovers entered the town of Dempsey...Yokum Parish. After a lame "yea, we're here" said in unison from all the people in the vehicle, Harry Sr. drove into the city of Dempsey. As Harry Sr. drove through downtown, Harry Jr. yelled "what a dump!" Harry Sr. tried to slap Harry Jr. in the backseat but spastically missed the boy who shouted "yes" that he had escaped this father's wrath this time. As Harry Sr. took a deep breath, he told Harry Jr. "I'll get you later boy!". Then, Harry Jr. told his father to hurry and stop so that his pet goat Festus, that was crated in a trailer being pulled by Harry Sr.'s truck, could get a water break. Harry Sr. rolled his eyes and told Jr. "That damn animal is gonna be sold when we get settled in Dempsey!" Jr. screamed, "Not my Festie! I love him!" Harry Sr. said, "you are too old to be falling all over that animal. It is ridiculous!" Then Harry Jr. pouted and Harry Sr. made a phone call. As they passed by Main Street, Harry Jr. would point to each business in the town and say "we will own you, we will own you...oh yea and we will own you!" His parents just smiled. Harry Jr. was quite the prognosticator on this day as the Conovers acquired much of the city within the next few years. The driving time from the Dallas, TX area was close to 8 hours and Harry Jr.'s father and mother had overdosed on their son who did not stay quiet for one minute during the entire trip when he was awake. They were both thankful that Harry Jr. slept most of the way to Dempsey. Before they arrived at their new house in Dempsey, Harry Sr. insisted that they stop at the local feed and hardware store to introduce himself. Harry Jr. pitched a bitch fit about having to stop, but Harry Sr. told him to "Shut It boy! After the stop at the local feed store, the Conovers finally made it to their new house. As Harry Sr. and Belle exited the truck their gait was quicker than usual. The quickness was attributed to Harry Jr. who followed closely behind. After sleeping at the new Dempsey house for the first night, the family drove to downtown Dempsey the next morning to check out the restaurants and shopping. Because it was Sunday, many shops were closed so the Conovers were not able to peruse the inside of the shops. It did not take long before Harry Jr. started complaining about being bored, hungry and tired. "My feet hurt bad" said Harry Jr. to his parents. His parents rolled their eyes at one another and told Harry Jr. to "suck it up". Since it was around lunchtime, the Conovers decided to have lunch in town. Harry Jr. picked a fast-food hamburger place that just opened in Dempsey a few months prior and was open on Sundays. His mother and father agreed to eat at the restaurant that Harry Jr. suggested although Harry Sr. complained about having gas from the bisquits and gravy Belle made for the family that morning. Belle said, "Sorry I cooked a breakfast that made you feel bad. But, you always complain that I never cook!" Harry Sr. said nothing to Belle's comment. After a couple of hours looking around the town, and hearing the loud rumble of Harry Sr.'s stomach, the Conovers returned home to an empty house and an uninhabited toilet for Harry Sr. The next Sunday, the Conovers decided to try the Sunday School at the Dempsey First Baptist Church. The pastor introduced the Conovers to the congregation and Belle and Harry Sr. were invited to join the church. Harry Jr. was invited to the young adult group, and he told his father that he would probably be bored with the group but maybe he should try it. Harry Jr said that maybe he could be inspirational to the other young adults. "You know maybe teach them something." Harry Jr. said. Belle joked with Harry Jr. and said "yes Harry, perhaps you can help the less fortunate and troubled youth because you have such a huge amount of compassion in your heart." Harry Jr. said "exactly!" seemingly not understanding that his mother was joking when she said Harry Jr. was compassionate. Harry Jr. became infamous in Dempsey as a know it all brat. Everyone knew who he was and knew that the boy was shallow and unkind. The new house in Dempsey, LA was beautiful. Made with clay bricks, the house had many angles and large windows. It was fashioned in a Frank Lloyd Wright designed home with three bedrooms and three-baths. The house had an exquisite garden in the back yard and was on a five-acre lot. As they entered the new house that Harry Sr. purchased when the family lived in Dallas. Belle walked around slowly inspecting the house giving it the white glove treatment without the white gloves. Harry Sr. was critical of some of the furnishings that had been ordered in Dallas, but the general consensus from the family is that they approved. Harry Jr. ran into the largest bedroom and jumped on the bed. Harry Sr. followed the boy and told him to "get off my bed boy!" Harry Jr. claimed the room and Harry Sr. asked him if he wanted to be slapped. Harry Sr. grabbed Harry Jr.'s arm and pulled him to the bedroom down the hall. He pushed him onto the bed in the next room that was close to he and Belle's and said "This is your room boy! You will sleep in this room and like it!" Harry Jr. told his dad that he was just joking and that he liked his room. There was very little negotiation with Harry's father. Jr. had tried in the past to change his father's mind about things, and it never worked. So, Harry Jr. started complimenting the room. Harry Sr. responded well to compliments so Harry Jr. proceeded to lay it on thick! "I really like the layout of the room Dad." Harry Jr. said in his most annoying suck-up voice. "Glad to hear it boy!" Harry

Sr. said. After unloading Harry Sr.'s truck, he noticed a wet stain on the seat where Harry Jr. sat on the trip. Harry Sr. yelled to Harry Jr. "Hey boy did you eat in my truck? I see a stain on the seat where you sat." Harry Jr. stammered and said "No, I didn't eat anything, but I had to go to the bathroom real bad so it could be a tiny slippage issue." Harry Sr. screamed and said "Are you telling me that you went to the bathroom on the seat of my truck boy! Harry Sr. yelled that it was not only unsanitary but disgusting for a boy his age to pee in his pants! How do you explain yourself Harry Jr.?" Harry Jr. paused quite a while as he was thinking of something to say. Then Harry Jr. blurted out "I meant that I spilled my drink on the seat. I'm sorry." Harry Jr. was lying. He had peed on the seat in his father's truck. He was too embarrassed to tell his father. Harry Jr.'s story change delighted his father who said "Well, okay. But, you have to watch it next time or I'm not gonna let you drink in my truck." Harry Jr. said "yes sir" to acknowledge his father and was pleased that he got away with this lie.

CHAPTER 10

THE NEW HOUSE
IN DEMPSEY

When the Conovers reached their new home in Dempsey, Jr. took Festus out of the crate in the back of the truck and put him in the fenced back yard. A building had been built specifically for Festus to stay in and Jr. proceeded to critique the quality of the building. He questioned the materials that were used and said to his father and mother "well, I guess Festie will like it. It isn't that large, but maybe he'll get used to it. Harry Sr. was visually furious at Jr.'s comments. He said "Well he isn't the smartest animal in the world so I think he will adjust Jr." Harry Jr. had developed a rather awkward relationship with Festus. He would try and hold the goat by his cloven hooves, and the clumsy goat would fall over himself. Harry Jr. thought he was taking good care of the goat. But, he did not brush the goat correctly. He brushed Festus so hard and so often that the animal would run at the site of the brush. When grooming the animal, Harry Jr. would brush the goat's mane against the direction of the animal's hair growth that is not recommended. And, instead of using a firm-bristled livestock brush that you can purchase at most livestock stores, Harry Jr. would use his mother's soft hairbrush on the animal's mane. Although Jr. never told his mother that he would use her brush to groom Festus,

Belle noticed that the brush contained some odd-looking hairs. Harry Jr. never understood why Festus didn't like his coat brushed, but he hurt the goat when he brushed him. Jr. called the goat Festie. The name made his father gag and his mother laugh. Jr.'s parents made fun of his conversations with the goat. They would call each other Festie and rub each other hands as if they were petting the goat. Jr. called the goat his brother and gave him inappropriate treats to eat like chocolate and oranges. When Festus laid down to rest, Harry Jr. would sit on his back and act like he was riding the goat. Harry Sr. thought that Harry Jr. was being sexual with the goat, and although Belle thought it looked odd, she did not agree with Harry Sr.'s sexual reference. The goat seemed confused and looked like he was wondering what the hell Harry Jr. was doing sitting on his back. The goat would raise its head, open its side-slanted eyes and make a bleat (like a baa sound). Although Harry Jr.'s love for the goat was short-lived until his boredom passed, his parents were happy that the goat kept Jr. out of their hair. When Harry Jr. played with Festus, his parents felt like they did not have to entertain the boy. Festus could keep Jr. engaged for a while eliminating the need for his parents to interact with the boy. The first week that the Conovers arrived in Dempsey, Harry Jr. told his parents that he wanted to have an informal session on raising a goat. Harry Sr. said to Belle "That boy didn't waste any time bugging us about that damn goat did he?" Belle acknowledged Harry Sr.'s question with a "no". The parents were not aware that Harry Jr. read incessantly about goats that prepared him for his "informal session next Sunday after church". Harry Sr. and Belle tried to discourage Harry Jr.'s information session on goats, but he pouted until the parents agreed to the presentation. Harry Jr. announced to the parents that the seminar would be held on the next Sunday at 1:00 after church. He said that they should meet him in the barn where Festus was staying when he wasn't in his crate. On Sunday, Harry Jr. promptly met his parents after church in their barn and led Festus to the center of the group as the "star pupil".

CHAPTER 11

JR'S PRESENTATION

Harry Jr. placed paper nametags on his mother and father and Festus. Harry Sr. said "we know the damn goat's name Jr." Belle said nicely, "well that is okay Jr. It is nice to include Festus in the group. The conversation is about him." Harry Sr. rolled his eyes at Belle's comment. The parents listened to Harry Jr. unenthusiastically. Harry Sr. was on the phone when the "seminar" started. Belle acted interested and rolled her eyes when Harry Sr. started talking on his phone. Belle said "Go ahead Harry Jr.. We can start and ignore the rude people in the room." Harry Jr. said "okay" and started his informational talk by explaining to at least one parent that "people think goats are dirty, but they are actually clean." Belle yawned but tried to shield her boredom with her hand. She thought that Harry Sr. needed to at least act like he was hearing Harry Jr.'s information. So, she swished her hand in front of Harry Sr.'s face. Harry Jr. continued. "Goats don't eat everything like people think. They are more interested in finding things not eating things." By then Harry Sr. was off his call and sarcastically commented "Wow, how could anyone live without this information." Belle said "zip it Harry Sr." Although both parents were bored with the information that Harry Jr. was presenting, Belle tried to act interested while Harry Sr. did not. After the information session on goats ended, Belle said emphatically "let's eat!" Harry Sr. then popped Belle on the butt and said "Can't miss a meal can ya Belly?" Belle excused herself to the bathroom where she blew her nose and wiped away a tear that was rolling down her right cheek. She had struggled with her body image all her life. Harry Sr. knew Belle's insecurities and disregarded her feelings. He was an insensitive and unkind man. The family had been in Dempsey for a week and the move had done nothing for the family other than to cement the animosity they felt for one another. The closeness that they experienced on the trip by sitting with each other was simply physical. Once the family exited the truck, they each walked their separate ways and did not communicate until dinner. Harry Sr. was obsessed with "his" farm in Dempsey and "his house" in Dempsey. He also thought that he would research Dempsey University and see if he might be interested in learning more about the farming and cattle industry by attending the local University in Dempsey. Harry Sr. did not have a college degree, and always felt inferior to the farming professionals that did. After moving to Dempsey, he applied to the University and was accepted, but never finished. He did have sex with a young girl from his animal science class, but he lost interest in the University after that. Fast forward to Dempsey, LA where the Conovers moved from Dallas. The population of Dempsey was about 220,245 people and was a very vibrant and diverse city. The city had a flagship university and affordable cost of living. Within a comfortable distance from Dempsey was a good opportunity to farm and raise cattle. Compared to Dallas, the Conovers felt like fish out of water in terms of culture and food. but, in time, they could easily call Dempsey their home. The general opinion of the Conovers in Dempsey was similar to how they were perceived in Dallas. Harry Sr. was considered a womanizer who was caught up in money and things he owned. Belle was considered quiet and very tolerant of an unfaithful man. And, Harry Jr.'s reputation from Dallas followed him to Dempsey. The residents in Dempsey thought that Jr was a manipulative and annoying brat. Little had changed since the Conovers moved to Dempsey. Harry Sr. continued to seek out young, attractive adulteresses and tried to recoup his youth, Belle carried her depressive mood to Dempsey and was standoffish with everyone but her family, and Harry Jr. strolled around the new city clueless as to what was happening in the world. Harry Sr. and Belle slept in separate beds and ate dinner alone on many occasions. They both knew they were not in love and only got married because of Harry Jr. They knew they were different and from opposite backgrounds. Belle was a voracious reader and lost herself in the literature she read. Harry Sr. could barely read and when he did read he was the king of misinterpretation. Belle quickly grew tired of Harry Sr.'s immaturity when they watched TV. Once, they were watching a documentary on Africa and Harry Sr. made a rude comment about the shirtless women who carry baskets on their heads. he would laugh and talk about the shirtless women's boobies as if he was watching a pornographic movie. Belle would explain to Harry Sr. that they carry the baskets on their heads because of the rough and rural terrain they were in. Harry would say "yea and I bet it kept their big boobies cool too" Belle would roll her eyes and ask Harry Sr. "why do you have to sexualize everything? Don't you have some work to do outside?" Then Harry Sr. would walk out of the house and slam the door. The residents who lived in the planned community where the Conovers lived found them to be pretentious and standoffish. Wealth had only been a lifelong experience for Harry Sr.. Belle's parents were not wealthy. Her family lived in a two-bedroom house in a medium income household about 56 miles from Dallas. Her city, Pilot Point, was a beautiful small town near Lake Ray Roberts. But, to Belle it was a small city with no opportunities. While living in Pilot Point, Belle shared a bedroom with her sister Pam. The sisters remained close until young Pamela's death from smallpox. After Pam died, Belle lost her best friend, Judith, to influenza. She and Judith were close in age and played together as young children in Pilot Point. The losses that Belle had experienced in her youth were pivotal in her life. After the loss of Pam and Judith, Belle found herself very depressed. She never had a close friend again. She was standoffish and leery of anyone who tried to be her friend. While in Pilot Point, Belle became a bitter and angry girl. At a young age and influenced by his father and mother, Harry Jr. became enamored with money in his young life. He showed no respect to his parents as it related to their wealth. While in Dallas, Harry Jr. would ask his parents "how much money will I get when you die? And, "what is in your will that is coming to me?" At night when Harry Sr. and Harry Jr.'s mother and father were getting ready for bed, Belle would ask Harry Sr. "What is wrong with that boy? He is so weird." The father would reply with a shrug and deep breath that "maybe he was dropped as a baby." Now, normally that comment would be a joke. But Harry Sr. was dead serious. Belle commented, "I don't remember dropping Harry Jr. on his head. I also don't remember any other person dropping Harry Jr. But, I do remember you beating the shit out of him one time." Harry Sr. replied "Oh, whipping the boy didn't cause him to be such a brat." And then, Belle and Harry Sr. turned off their bedside lights that were engraved with their names and went to sleep. They never enjoyed being parents. Belle and Harry Sr. liked to travel and would take trips often when Harry Jr,. was growing up. They never called to check on him when they were on vacation. They never brought him a souvenir from the place they had visited. Harry Jr., was virtually raised by his house-keeper, Rosa, who did not speak much English. Communicating with her was difficult, but Harry Jr. liked Rosa because she wasn't judgmental probably because she never understood what Jr. was saying. As he grew up, Harry Jr. would tell the story to other boys about seeing Rosa's breasts. It was Harry Jr.'s first insight into sexuality. Rosa was changing her shirt after spilling grease on herself from the empanadas she was making for Harry Jr. There was a crack in the door of her bedroom, and Harry Jr. found the opportunity to take a quick look at Rosa changing her shirt. Rosa did not know that Harry Jr. was looking at her, but she would not have approved. As the years rolled by, Harry Jr. grew up in Dempsey. Although he spent many school years in Dallas, he ultimately finished high school in Dempsey with few friends and people who did not care for him. His father tried to get Harry Jr. interested in football and other sports, but Harry Jr. was a lazy kid who did not ever play on a sports team and showed no interest in any sport. He liked to doodle with the internet and play games on his computer. But, he would always read the cheater clues and win. So, the boy was not challenged and grew bored easily. Jr. liked to help his father on the farm, but he had very low energy that always turned into a fight with Harry Sr. His father would scream at Harry Jr. and ask him "Why Harry? Why can't you walk 500 feet without breaking a sweat? You are young...not like me. I just do not understand your lack of energy!" Harry Jr. would reply "I have a hard time breathing because I have asthma." Harry Sr. rolled his eyes at Harry Jr. and told Belle "That boy just doesn't have it. I know he has asthma but jessum!" Belle would say "yes, I know. Sometimes people do things that we just cannot control Harry and we really don't deserve." Belle was referring to Harry Sr.'s infidelity, and he knew it." This was the first time that Belle had mentioned Harry Sr.'s affairs. At that point, Harry Sr. stuttered and stammered around the comment. He changed the subject quickly. They were both acting awkward around each other. Harry Sr. totally ignored Belle's comment and acted like he had not heard her. Both understood that infidelity had almost ruined their marriage, but as more time passed the subject was never broached again. Over the years, Belle stopped caring about being close to Harry Sr.. She was tired and had reached the decision that her bad marriage was her destiny. Oh, she would reminisce about past lovers, but the memories stayed in her past. The truth was that Belle and Harry Sr. had a terrible relationship and one that probably should have ended a long time ago. Belle was not enough for Harry Sr. and Harry Sr. was not enough for Belle McFadden Conovers. But, Belle sadly thought that it would be harder to end it than to just stay in it. So, she stayed married to Harry Sr. and was unhappy all of her life. When she felt unloved, Belle would ask Harry Sr. "Why did you even marry me Harry? You are obviously not attracted to me and hate our child." Harry Sr. would say, "You are my best-friend Belley. I like Jr.. He is just super annoying". Belle would say "Yes, he is, but he is the only family we have left so you might as well try and enjoy him." Harry Sr. would simply say "yea, your right." Harry Sr. was a serial cheat who had now started screwing an 18-year-old check-out girl at the Piggly Wiggly in Dempsey. Her name was Dafney and she was a voracious sexual woman who agreed to sleep with Harry Sr. without hesitation. Dafney and Harry Sr. thought that no one knew that they were sleeping together. But, everyone in Dempsey knew that they were having an affair. Dafney's parents went to the same church that Harry Sr. was a member, and her father and mother were in the same Sunday school class as Harry Sr. and Belle. Her parents and Harry Sr. spoke openly about his affair with Daffney and told Harry Sr. "just don't go and knock her up." Apparently, Dafney had seen another married man prior to Harry Sr. and had an abortion. The man Dafney was seeing and sleeping with before Harry Sr. was Belle's friend's husband. Belle would talk to her friend at church about the affair but had no idea that Harry Sr. would be Dafney's next sexual partner. At this point, Harry Sr. acknowledged the peculiar situation that he was in and the potential problem it could very well cause him with Belle. One day he said to Dafney, "Well Dafney, I think it is about time to call this quits." This situation is a little too close to home and I cannot risk my wife finding out about you and me." Dafney would tell Harry Sr in her country drawl "Sure is a small world ain't it Harry." referring to the connections that the couple seemed to have between her parents and Harry and Belle. Harry Sr. would say "yea it sure as hell is Dafney." He cringed a the thought of the coincidence with his relationship to Dafney. Harry Sr. then wiped the perspiration from his brow that had developed during their conversation. Harry Sr. thought to himself, "I've got to end this relationship quick." After Harry Sr. explained to Dafney that they could not see each other anymore, Dafney threatened to tell Belle about the affair. "My parents already know that we are involved so it would not be difficult for Belle to find out that you are screwing around on her...with me." Dafney then said, "Wouldn't that be a hoot for your wife to find out that her friend's daughter is screwing her husband?" Harry Sr. said "yea that would be some kind of hoot!" Then, Harry Sr. offered Dafney a few thousand dollars to keep her mouth zipped about the affair. Dafney in her manipulative way told Harry Sr. "Well Harry, I think my body is worth more than just a few thousand dollars. I think it is worth at least $10,000." Harry Sr. chocked on his saliva and said to Dafney "I suppose so. I need some time to get the money from the bank though. I am going to have to hide this from Belle and it will take a few days." Dafney responded "Well, don't let it take too long hon. I have a great memory so I won't forget what we have been doing for a few months." Shortly after Belle had heard the rumor about Dafney and Harry Sr., she confronted him about the rumor. He denied the rumor as he had done before. But, Belle told him that she is friends with a lady who is married to someone who has been intimate with a young girl named Dafney. Belle's allegiance to a man who was unfaithful and cruel to her was well-known among Dempsey residents. The people of Dempsey thought that Harry Sr. was a perv, and they tried their best to keep their children away from him. Within the next couple of years, Harry Sr.'s friend and his wife Susan bought a new house in Dempsey around the same neighborhood as Harry Sr. and Belle. Their house, although nice, was less opulent than Harry and Belle's house. Patrick had agreed to help Harry Sr. develop his farm and manage his livestock. Belle wasn't super keen on the idea of having Harry Sr.'s friend and wife living in their community, but she thought that perhaps they could help out with the farm wand help with Jr. Belle never really cared for Susan. She thought that Susan was nosey and intrusive.. After the Conovers had been in Dempsey for a few years, Harry Sr. traded Jr.'s goat to a farmer who needed help with brush control in Dempsey. Festus just disappeared one day, and Harry Jr. did not know where he was or if he was dead or alive. He was devastated…an emotion that Harry Jr. seemed to never show. Harry Sr. told Jr. "I told you that when we moved to Dempsey I was gonna get rid of Festus, and I did. You are too old for a pet like Festus." Crying, Jr. pitched a hissy and threw himself on the grass. Belle said "Harry, that boy is going to hurt himself throwing his body on the ground like that!" Harry Sr. simply said "oh well." During Harry Jr.'s childhood in Dempsey, he would beg his parents to have another child. His mother said "no way!" His father would agree. Harry Jr.'s parents never had another child and secretly regretted having Harry Jr.. Harry Sr. and Belle were both raised by parents who believed that children were simply a prize to show off to their friends…not trouble-making little brats. Although Belle was kinder than Harry Sr. as a parent, she certainly would not have scored high on the parent test. She was cold and stern and very bitter towards Harry Sr. who had been nothing but cruel to her. As Harry Jr. walked down the streets of Dempsey, people would move to the other side of the street to avoid engaging with him. He never caught on to the fact that he was disliked and avoided by people in Dempsey. When people crossed the street to avoid running into Harry Jr., he would cross the street to make sure he ran into them so they would have to talk to him. Harry Jr. did not have a delete button in his brain to take back any awkward comment he would say to anyone he encountered on the streets of Dempsey. As a student at Dempsey High School, Harry Jr. tried to make friends, but he wasn't very successful and was inappropriate. If he met someone that he liked and wanted to be their friend, Harry Jr. would say "Want to be my friend?" The person he asked to be his friend thought that Harry Jr. was a weirdo and left quickly from the conversation. He wasn't even successful making friends with the dorky unpopular students. The young girls, even the most unattractive girls were grossed out by Harry Jr.'s overly effeminate behavior and pasty skin. The young boys that attended school with Harry Jr., thought that Jr. was queer and awkward. Harry Jr. struggled to pass his classes. He was a know it all, but he didn't know the right "all". He turned his homework in late and had a tutor who ended up quitting when Harry Jr. tried to teach the tudor math. Harry Jr. was not active in sports and disliked any kind of extracurricular activity that required exercise. He preferred to take naps when he wanted and not interact with the teaching staff. Harry's mother and father did not seem to care that Harry Jr. was lax in school. Harry Sr. told Harry Jr. "I understand that people don't get you. Hell, hey don't get me either. You are rare and special, like me. People just don't understand us. Harry Sr. continued "But Jr. you have to give the teachers what they want. Then they will leave you alone. So, do your homework and suck up to the teachers okay?" Harry Jr. turned to his dad and said "Okay dad. I am a pro at sucking up!" His dad said "I know you are Harry Jr... I know you are." The people in Dempsey never warmed up to Harry Jr. He was excluded from parties, kicked out of academic clubs and never invited to his classmates houses. In the library, he would speak loudly and laugh obnoxiously. As he walked down the city streets of Dempsey, he would throw his trash on the ground and steal mail out of the mailboxes of people who lived in Dempsey. Although Harry's parents were embarrassed by their son's bad behavior, they fake talked him up to their friends. Instead of disciplining Harry Jr., Harry Sr. would complement the child on his passion to be himself and strength as a person. Although the Conovers put on a happy and strife free demeanor with everyone they met in Dempsey, anger was a common condition in the Conovers' house. Harry's father was angry at Harry Jr.'s mother. Harry Jr.'s mother was angry at Harry Sr.. Harry Jr.'s parents were angry at him and Harry Jr. was just plain angry at everything and everyone. The Conovers never took responsibility for any of their negative behavior. If something went wrong in their family, the Conovers' blamed someone else for their misfortune and never took accountability for their behavior. Regarding Harry Jr., Harry Sr. and Belle would ask themselves "why does Harry Jr. act so angry and strange." They never reached a consensus on the boy's weirdness. The parents would just agree that it just was the way it was. Harry Sr. and Belle Conovers were frequent travelers and often left Harry behind with sitters when they were away on a trip. They did not pay much attention to Harry when they were at home and admitted to escaping the drudgery of parenthood via travel. Harry Jr.'s mother never wanted to have children but felt like she should since all her women friends were having babies. Harry Sr. was apathetic to having children, but he was intimidated by Harry's mother and succumbed to her "need to have a child". Harry Jr. never received the attention or love from his parents. He grew up feeling insecure, irrelevant and unwanted. After moving to Dempsey, Harry Sr. applied for school at Dempsey State University. He had never attended college and thought that taking classes in agricultural management and farming could benefit him in Dempsey. Additionally, a friend of Harry Sr. gave him a tip that Dempsey was the new money-making property in the country. Harry Sr. chose to attend college in Dempsey to help him with agriculture management and farming. The college had a very strong program in agriculture management. After applying to Dempsey University, Harry Sr. was accepted. He would start during the summer session after arriving to Dempsey from Dallas. He entered the college as an older student which he hated and took classes in farming, animal, dairy, and poultry sciences. In time, Harry Sr. thought he was smarter than all the other classmates because he was older and "more experienced in farming than the other students. Belle told him to not be cocky and that he might be surprised at the level of knowledge the other students held. At that comment, Harry let out a burp and said "no way". Then Belle zipped it. Harry Sr. started school excited about learning strategies on how to be a profitable farmer and create productive crops. But then, he bored quickly and never graduated from the Dempsey University proclaiming it was a school for "wannabees and has beens." It was good enough for Jr. who would eventually graduate from the school. Harry Sr. felt like he knew enough and learned enough to propel himself into a profitable business of farming and raising cattle without graduating from Dempsey U. Unfortunately, Harry Sr. was grossly over-confident in his farming knowledge. He lost many crops from assuming things that were incorrect. He also lost cattle from assuming things that were incorrect. Of course, he would never admit it was his lack of knowledge to blame. He was excellent at blaming everyone else for his "bad luck". Belle felt isolated and had trouble meeting people in the new city. Harry Sr. did not pay much attention to Belle, and she felt neglected. It took an already strained relationship with Harry Sr. to a new level when the family moved to Dempsey. Harry Sr. was an absentee husband and father. He would leave his house and not return for days. The rumor was that he was having an affair with a divorced lady in town. Her name was Ellen. She was unlike Harry Sr.'s other affairs. She was an affluent divorcee from Dallas who moved to Dempsey for a shot at a new life. She had money and was more refined than Harry Sr.'s exes. The couple grew close quickly and Harry Sr. was smitten. Ellen had two sons close in age with Jr. The boys attended private college in Dallas which was paid for by their dad, an affluent attorney and partner in the law firm Colby, Anderson and Brewer in Dallas. Harry

Jr. knew of the affair and was awkwardly expected to meet Ellen's boys when the Conover's traveled to Dallas to pick up more of their belongings. When Harry Jr. met Ellen's sons, he thought that they were snobby and ultra preppy boys who had no place in his life. Harry Sr. spent an enormous time trying to convince Jr. to like the boys. Junior wasn't having it. He loved his mother and thought that his dad was a horrible man. Ellen and Harry Sr. were playing house and acted as if they were high school sweethearts. As Harry Sr. continued his affair with Ellen, it was time for Jr. to be enrolled in high school. His parents enrolled him in Dempsey High School. Jr had already developed a rather abrasive reputation in the town of Dempsey. The arguing and fighting reached a boiling point between Jr.'s mother and father. Harry Sr. was completely smitten with Ellen and wanted to marry her. Belle felt lost and did not know what to do. She wasn't happy but trapped in a loveless marriage to a man who had yet again chose someone other than herself. It was around this time that Belle fell down the hallway stairs at the Conovers' house. She did not die, but the injury caused severe brain damage that forced her into an assisted living facility in Dempsey now, Belle felt helpless. She was bedridden and extremely depressed. Scared to be alone...scared to be divorced...scared of Harry Sr., Belle was not getting better after months. No one visited her and, she had developed pressure ulcers from lying in the bed so long. The nurses at the long-term facility felt sorry for Belle. They would rotate among themselves to sit and talk to Belle. That only worked for a short time. The nurses would talk among themselves and say "That Harry Sr. is a real bastard!" The medical staff at the long-term facility where Belle was staying always reference Belle as the "woman with the bastard of a husband and an uncaring family." Harry Sr. was very vocal to Ellen about his unhappy marriage. He often called Belle a cow and unloveable. He rarely visited Belle in the facility and acted bored when he was there. Belle could not move the lower half of her body and Harry Sr. was not interested...he did not care. None of Belle's church friends visited her and Jr. only visited her occasionally. Generally, she was left alone in the assisted living facility for the duration of her time there. Harry Jr. was a senior at the high school in Dempsey and had started looking at college options. He was considering applying at Dempsey University. Although he frequently dreamt of the day he would leave his family home, Jr. was a fearful boy who wanted to stay close to home. He would use his mother's injury as a reason to stay close to home. Harry Sr. was the primary suspect in Belle's fall. It was not a secret that he wanted to marry the women (Ellen) he was having an affair so it wasn't a stretch to think Harry Sr. had something to do with Belle's fall. Ellen and Harry Jr. met at a men's clothing store where she worked in Dempsey. If you could say one thing positive about Ellen it was that she was the least sleazy woman that Harry Sr. chose to cheat with. Ellen and Harry Sr. had things in common. They both moved to Dempsey from Dallas, and each had children who were the same age and all boys. Also, Ellen's children were deciding what college they would attend. Ellen's sons wanted to attend college in Dallas. Harry Jr. did not want to go to college but felt pressured to attend based on past comments that his parents had made to him. Ellen's sons chose Southern Methodist University...a private college in Dallas that was a nationally ranked private school and a global research facility. The on-campus cost estimate for SMU was about $80,000...compared to Dempsey University a public college that was estimated to cost about $41,000 for non-Dempsey residents including housing. Ellen and her children were accustomed to the finer things in life, and her boys were snooty. The boy's father and Ellen's ex-husband was a partner in a prominent Dallas law firm so she and her children were used to the finer things in life. Ellen and Harry Sr. acted like they were a family and Ellen, although still a resident of Dallas, would visit Dempsey often and stayed weeks at a time. Belle was out of sight and out of mind for Harry Sr. as she spent her days and nights in the nursing home fighting for her life. Harry Sr. of course never mentioned Belle to Ellen or Ellen to Belle and planned to divorce Belle as quickly as possible. Ellen was wealthy and Harry Sr. liked the money she had and saw potential in getting richer from his relationship with Ellen. But, Ellen was not that convinced that Harry Sr. was the right stock for her. He was not an intelligent or groomed man. But, she was scared to be alone so she stayed with Harry Sr. Harry Sr. thought Ellen to be top notch and full of class. He believed that the closer he became to Ellen perhaps her influence, money, and class would rub off on him. Harry Sr. was being investigated for Belle's fall down the stairs and was interviewed by several law enforcement professionals. His reputation in Dempsey as an unfaithful spouse did not do anything for him. Prior to being questioned for Belle's accident, Harry Sr. died of a massive heart attack. He left a grieving adulteress, an incapacitated wife and an ungrateful son who barely knew the time of day. Unfortunately, no one would pay the price for Belle's fall down the stairs. Prior to his death Harry Sr., asked Ellen to marry him. She thought he was a buffoon. He was already married. And, he had nothing to offer Ellen that she did not already have. Of course, the proposal was simply a gesture since he was already legally married to Belle. But, Harry felt very much in love with Ellen and told his pastor at church that he had made a terrible decision when he married Belle. Although Ellen was flattered by Harry Sr.'s offer and a little sad that he died, she was determined to never marry again, and had he been alive, she certainly would not have married Harry Sr. He wasn't polished enough for Ellen, and he did not come from the right social stock. In addition, when Ellen found out that Harry Sr. was a prime suspect in Belle's fall, she started to aggressively pull away from Harry and was set on ending the relationship. Belle's fall reminded Ellen of a conversation that she had with Harry at the height of their relationship. Harry Sr. confessed to Ellen that during one of Harry Sr. and Belle's arguments he was tempted to throw Belle down the stairs. A stunning admission of guilt from Harry Sr. who said that he was kidding but seemed serious to Ellen. The admission sent chills down Ellen's spine, and she became scared of Harry Sr. after that comment In order to close the case on Belle's fall, the police interviewed Harry Jr. about his father's possible involvement in his mother's accident. Conditioned to fear the retribution of his father, Harry Jr. attempted to clear Harry Sr.'s name in the case of his mother's fall. Harry Jr. played two sides of the story and blamed both parents for the argument. Harry Jr. told the prosecutor that his mother was unhappy and frequently hit his father without cause. The accusation was not true. He also told the prosecutor that his mother would run around the house naked screaming at his father for no reason. This was also untrue. Harry Jr. had practiced talking to the prosecutor about his parents. He would stand in front of the mirror in a suit and tie and practice lying to the police. Then, in an effort to get on his mother's good side, Harry Jr. would visit her in the long-care nursing facility and hold up a note explaining what had happened with the prosecutor. Harry Jr. was playing a cruel game with both of his parents by playing sides against each other. Although his accusations really didn't matter since his father was dead, he felt some personal vengeance against his father. Jr. explained to his mother that he told the police that Harry Sr. beat his mother and was unfaithful throughout the entire marriage. And, he also told his mother that he told the police that Harry Sr. pushed her down the stairs. Harry's mother smiled a crooked paralyzed smile when he told her that Harry Sr. was being questioned for her accident. She smiled bigger than Harry Jr. had ever seen. She then patted him on the head and died. Harry Jr. said out loud "well I guess that is that. After Belle died from the fall, Harry Sr. was the person who would always be blamed for her death. The death became somewhat of a tall tale to new residents of Dempsey. Harry Sr. became a bigger than life scrooge who killed his wife and made Belle a sad memory. Harry Jr. lived years in Dempsey haunted by the memory of his father and mother. He attended Dempsey University where he majored in computer science and was somewhat of an isolate. He rarely went outside of his house and played on the computer constantly. After the death of Harry Jr.'s mother and father, Harry Sr.'s best-friend in high school Patrick and his wife Susan became Harry Jr.'s guardians. Harry Sr.'s legal paperwork from his will authorized that the couple move into the new house that Harry Sr. had bought for his family when they were in Dallas. The couple agreed to Harry Sr.'s request when he was alive to look after Harry Jr. until he was in college. The legal paperwork for the purchase of the land had been completed prior to Harry Sr.'s death, and Harry Sr. had revised his will years ago to include his best-friend and his wife as the guardian of Harry Jr. Harry Jr. was already in the house with his things when his father had died. So, he felt like his dad's friends Patrick and Susan were jumping rather quickly into his father's house. Immediately after Harry Sr.'s friend and wife moved into the house, Harry Jr. was given their house rules that included his curfew, and his weekly chores. Jr. never liked Patrick and Susan. The couple had become the objects of fights between Jr.'s dad and mom. Jr.'s dad would spend an inordinate time trying to sell the couple to Belle, and Belle never liked Patrick or Susan. His father played two sides of the coin. At times he would tell his family that the couple were gold diggers and used people for what they could get from them. So, Jr. was opposed to being told what to do by his father's "user friends." One of Jr.'s responsibilities was to clean out his guardian's cat litter box. He told Susan that he refused to complete this chore because of his asthma. In his typical dramatic, theatrical manner he told her that cleaning out the cat's litter box would produce a major asthma attack. Jr. said, "It isn't even my cat. I hate cats. Why do I have to clean up behind your cat?" Susan replied "Because I am your parental guardian and you will do what I say. Or, your non-compliance will result in a lower allowance. Do you understand me...Jr.?" After rolling his eyes, he said to Susan, "I am quite taken back by your aggressiveness. I do not see how my father would agree with you. And, why do you talk to me as if you are my employer and I am your subordinate?" Susan replied "Well, the situation that we are in is kind of like a professional work environment. Your father trusted me and Patrick to look after you and the house he bought for your family, and you will abide by our rules!" Harry Jr. said "bull shit!" as he stomped to his room and slammed the door. Then he pitched a bitch fit and threw the papers on his desk all over the room. Susan followed closely behind and told him to "Pick up the damn papers." The two never got along. They constantly interrupted each other and pitted Harry Sr.'s best friend Patrick against each other. Jr. replied "I am not going to clean out YOUR cat's litter box. You can dock my allowance all you want. I have my own bank account with my money secure in it!" The conversation ended on a gloomy note and nothing was resolved. Harry Jr. never emptied the cat box, and continued to break curfew. Jr. dreamt of the day he could walk out of Susan andPatrick's life forever. After Harry Jr. went to his room, he became aware that he should probably be open for the couple's suggestions. Jr. thought "This is how I'll get what I want. Dad told me that." Since Harry Jr. loved money, he agreed to what Susan and Patrick required of him except for the cat's litter box. The box sat undisturbed and uncleaned until Susan finally cleaned it. The couple tried to take Jr. under their wing and mold him into what they thought he should be. But, Harry Jr. would not have it. He would pitch a temper tantrum like he did when he was in grade school. Harry Jr. gave them hell. He would not follow their rules for curfew...not clean the cat's litter box....and do very little to help his Dad's best-friend work the fields that was primarily why Harry Sr. asked Patrick to look after Harry Jr. Often, Harry Jr. would exceed the guardian's curfew by hours. He did not necessarily have any reason to have a curfew. He had few friends to do anything with and if he was asked to go get a burger in town with a classmate, he refused. So, he would sit outside of his house many times past curfew to simply piss his guardians off. Jr. often accused Patrick and Susan of trying to act like his parents. And they would say "Yes, you are right. We act like your parents because your father asked us to take care of you! And, tough if you don't like it!" After a while, Harry Jr. won the battle between Patrick and Susan. They stopped acting like they cared for the boy and essentially let him do what he wanted to do. They all eventually fell into normalcy and became housemates and left each other alone. Jr. continued to refuse to help around the house or help with his father's farming business. Until, one day Patrick suggested that he and Harry Jr. work on a building project together. Patrick explained to Jr. that he needed a building to keep the tools used to farm the land. Harry Jr. was surprised and interested in the project especially when his uncle told him that it was "Jr.'s project" to direct. This was Harry Sr.'s dream…for Harry Jr. and Patrick to work together to make his land profitable. Patrick and Susan had no children of their own, and the couple never showed any interest in having a child. Despite their disinterest in childbirth, Harry Sr., a terrible father and someone who never wanted a child talked children up to Patrick and Susan who never responded well to his endorsement of parenthood. Harry Jr. was a terrible example of why a couple should have children. If anything, Jr.'s behavior was the exact reason why Patrick and Susan looked down on being a parent. The couple learned that they would never have a child after parenting Harry Jr.. The aunt referred to Harry Jr. as the "demon child" and after assisting in raising Harry Jr. they were relieved to make a final decision of no children. Harry Jr., Patrick and Susan never formed a bond with Harry Jr. Harry Jr. always felt like there was some weirdness in how Patrick and Susan talked about his father. It was as if there was some kind of secret among the three that existed. Then one rare Friday night Harry Jr., Susan and Patrick pulled out the photo albums, opened a bottle of wine that Harry Sr. had purchased for the couple years ago and popped the cork. Although Harry Jr. was not the legal age yet to drink, the couple allowed him to have a small glass of wine. Since none of them were frequent drinkers, they became tipsy quickly. The wine hit each of them like a led balloon and all of them became silly and talkative. Harry Jr. saw an opportunity to ask them about the couple's relationship with his father. Although slightly apprehensive, Susan explained that Harry Sr. made a pass at her shortly after she met him. She said they were at a movie theater, and he put his hand up her skirt. "It was dark in the theater so no one could see what he was doing. I mean Patrick was sitting right beside me, and your father made the move. "The gaul of that man…right in front of his best-friend" Susan said in a slurred voice! She continued, "Things were never the same with your father or your mother. I told your mother about the incident and that your father asked me if I wanted to have sex. She shrugged and told me that sounded like something Harry Sr. would do". "She acted like it was normal! Can you believe that?" Susan continued. Harry Jr. quickly said "yes, I completely believe it. My father was unfaithful to my mother throughout their marriage. He actually told me and probably my mother that he wanted to marry one of the women he was seeing. Had he lived longer he probably would have married her." Susan then told Harry Jr. that she told Patrick about the overture, and he said "I will never speak to that bastard again!" For years we never had any contact with your mother or father. "That is why you never saw us Jr. Then, one Sunday your father called Patrick. Harry Sr. said nothing about what I claimed he did, and the friends started talking again. So, consequently we started talking again to your parents after years. Of course nothing was resolved, and I was a little pissed off that Patrick did not say anything about the pass your father made at me. But then, I let it to.

Life's too short you know? Patrick and I spoke about the incident one time and then never again. Harry Sr. was the older friend and bullied Patrick terribly during their childhood. They attended the same school and Harry Sr. told Patrick to not tell anyone he was Patrick's friend. That did not faze Patrick who tried to win Harry Sr.'s affection and attention for a long time. I suppose your father had a moment when he missed talking to his best-friend and then called us." Harry Jr. had a "ah hah" moment and said to himself "I knew something had happened between my father and Patrick. Then he snapped his fingers and said "I'm right again!" He said this outloud. Disgusted, Susan remembered why she couldn't stand Jr. she said to herself "that is exactly why I think that little bastard Jr. is a bad seed!" During editing his will, Harry Sr. told Harry Jr. that he was going to make plans to have his friends Patrick and Patrick's wife Susan take care of Jr. when he died. Jr. pleaded with his father to not make Susan and Patrick guardians of him when he died "Please dad don't do this. Susan is a bitch, and Patrick's breath could kill a cow. Harry Sr. said to Jr. "suck it up son! This is what responsible parents do when they are creating a will. They make sure that their children are looked after when their parents are gone." After that discussion Jr. said "well, I guess that is that." It was time for Harry Jr. to pre-register at Dempsey University and so he decided to go online and order some new clothing. Harry Jr. spent about a $1,000 dollars on clothes. Instead of City Outfitters collegiate collections that many college kids wore, Harry Jr. bought his clothes from expensive stores: He used on-line stores like Tom Ford, SAKS, Chanel and Georgio Armani to purchase his school clothes. The bow tie, that is avoided by many college students was among his favorite. His shoes were always polished, his hair always trimmed and his nails always manicured…yes, manicured.

CHAPTER 12

JR.'S FIRST DAY
OF COLLEGE

On his first day, Harry drove to the college in his father's BMW that he was given after his father died. His flagrant excessiveness did not serve him well among his classmates at Dempsey U. He was immediately perceived by his classmates as a snob and conceited. He was ultra-preppy and would roam the halls at Dempsey University with a better than you attitude" and greet other students with a ridiculous "hidey ho or bonjour." Over the next few years, Jr. evaded fights by hiding in the bathroom standing on the toilet in his penny loafers and Ralph Lauren Knit Pique' blazer that he purchased for almost $600.00. He would use a foreign accent when he spoke because he thought it made him sound affluent. Most of the students at Dempsey U were from all over the world. Jr. made negative comments about students from the Midwest and asked them "do you live on a farm?" an obvious negative assumption by uninformed people. Then he would ask students from places like Kenya or Uganda "have you ever been on a safari?" Jr. was ignorant and rude. From his freshman year at Dempsey U to his junior year when he met Liza Roberts, Harry Jr. did his very best at grossing out the females in his classes to threatening the males. He did not believe in working on himself to improve his relationships because his motto was "you can't improve perfection," a self-described personal assessment. So, he dealt with the alienation from his classmates along with the rejected date offers and the wedgies that he was frequently given by his male counterparts. One day Harry Jr. went to the college bookstore to buy a book that was recommended by his economics teacher. As he entered the bookstore, Harry Jr. saw a young woman sitting quietly at a desk reading a book called "The Bell Jar". Her name was Liza Roberts, and she was a homely kind of gal who had a part-time job in the bookstore. She was a junior at Dempsey U, like Harry Jr., with a degree in Library Science or what Harry Jr. rudely called "an easy peasy degreasy". Liza's role was to catalog the books and organize subject matter. She was plain but well-groomed and interesting in a bookworm kind of way. The book she was reading was written by Sylvia Platt and was dark but appropriate considering Liza was smart but dark. Harry entered the library and became focused on Liza. In a particularly talkative day, like most days, Harry Jr. approached Liza. He recognized the book from his childhood home in the great room corner stashed away. It was his mother's, and he was not sure if she had read the book but assumed not. Then Harry screamed out "The Bell Jar! What a stupid name for a book!" Liza rolled her eyes and adjusted herself in her chair. She said nothing but shook when Harry Jr. screamed loudly in her direction "Hi... hey" said Harry in his outside voice. Liza jumped and almost choked on the sandwich she was eating at her desk. Then, Harry grabbed the sandwich out of Liza's hand and took a big bite out of it. Liza thought "Boy, he didn't have to grab the sandwich. I would have given him a bite." But, Harry wasn't hungry...he was just rude. Liza never met Harry but had met the type of guy he was before this day. He was over-confident, a ladies' man, and a real rat of a person. Then Harry Jr. sat down by Liza without being asked and patted her left thigh. Liza thought that Harry Jr. touching her leg was extremely presumptuous since they had never met. Then Harry Jr. said to Liza, "Harry Conover Jr. here.". Liza thought, "What an asshole!" Then Harry said "Well, you must think I am an asshole." Liza lied and said, No, of course not." with two fingers criss-crossed behind her back implying the lie. Although Liza was not impressed with Harry and his obnoxious demeanor, she was flattered that he showed interest in her since it was a rare occurrence in her life. She thought that Harry was self-assured and confident, two characteristics that she lacked but envied. She thought his move to grab her sandwich was lame. But, Liza was surprisingly interested in him for his boldness and confidence. She explained where she was from, why she chose Dempsey U. (strong library science curriculum) and that her father was very sick and her mother was pretty much occupied with taking care of him. Harry explained that both his parents were deceased but he was independent on his own. "I am the King of Me" Harry Jr. explained to Liza. He explained to Liza that he was living with his father's best friend and wife in Dempsey since his father named the couple his parental custodians through his dad's will. Regardless of their parental guidance label, I am pretty independent and do what I want." After the two chitchatted a bit, Harry then asked Liza if she wanted to have dinner with him on Friday. He thought that she seemed desperate enough to accept a date with him. And, he was pleasantly surprised when she said "yes". The truth was that he was much more desperate than she. His success rate on dates was not good, and Harry was unreasonably self-confident and accomplished at convincing a woman that she really wanted to do what she didn't think she wanted to do. He would use his signature bull-shit to create interest from someone from the opposite sex. He would use "the book" that he bought in jr. high school to manipulate women into going out with him. The book had a five-part description as to how to act when you wanted to date someone. #1: Gain trust #2: Act like someone who cares about potential date's opinion #3 Put the potential dates's priorities first. #4 Be kind and listen to potential date's needs and desire# 5 Leave your ego at home. Harry Jr. had asked Liza for a date. She normally did not accept a dinner invitation on such short notice. But, but she was strangely intrigued by Harry Jr. He wasn't very attracted to Liza nor she to him, but Harry Jr. was odd and so was Liza. Harry Jr. was more of an experiment to Liza. She thought that she could learn something from Harry Jr. So Liza accepted the date with Harry Jr. privately hoping that her acceptance was not an error. Then Liza thought "my mother has warned me about men like Harry Jr. who is overly self-confident and a braggart. But, my mother doesn't know it all and look who she picked! Her mother's words reverberated in her ears. Her mother would say, "There are those boys out there Liza who will treat you like an animal, use you for what they can get from you, and then dump you in the trash." Although Liza's mom's words were harsh, Liza drew a cold chill hoping that she was wrong about Harry Jr. and the person her mom assumed he was. In spite, of her apprehension, Liza agreed to the date with Harry Jr. She thought if nothing else it would be entertaining. After giving Harry her phone number, he joked with Liza and asked her "It isn't a fake number is it?" Liza rolled her eyes and said "of course not" although she thought privately "maybe it should be." Liza had been on just a few dates so she was not sure what was considered normal dating questions. But, her gut told her that Harry Conover was not normal nor was his demeanor. She had read about men like Harry. Men who used women for what they could get. Men who were rude to women and thought that women were intellectually below them. Liza was in touch with who she was. She also knew that men were not particularly attracted to her. She was smart but kind of a wallflower who was not outgoing at all. Liza was quiet, plain and awkward. She was pretty in her own way. She was not flashy...not sexual but plain and with strong solid features and a smart intellect that many men found interesting. She also had a strong build and was not at all a weakling. But, she could be awkward. When her date would try and kiss her goodnight, she would giggle like a child. Other times she would scream like a madwoman when her date would try to touch her in a way she deemed inappropriate. Her snorting laugh and constant nail biting turned people off. Around Dempsey U., Liza Roberts reputation was that she was very odd and difficult to get to know. Her nickname was "stinky fish" because one of the boys in her class saw her smell her fingers after pulling a loose string that was underneath her armpit on her shirt. She would argue that she was simply trying to get rid of the string, but the nickname stuck. Harry was not aware of her nickname until one of the boys in his class called him "fish lover" after his dinner with Liza. When he later learned of the nickname, he understood it after having dinner with Liza. Harry called Liza on Thursday night to confirm the date for Friday. He asked her for directions to her off campus apartment and finalized a time that he would pick her up. It was an odd conversation as Liza acted as if she knew nothing about the date. Harry was befuddled and asked Liza if she remembered accepting his invitation and meeting him at the college bookstore. Liza said "oh yea". They agreed to dinner at 7:00 on Friday night. Harry asked Liza if she liked Italian food. She said "yes". Harry said inappropriately "Well, I'm glad you do because that is the only restaurant where I made a reservation." Liza uncomfortably laughed and said "well that's good". Harry picked Liza up on Friday night and honked his horn in front of her apartment to let her know he was outside. Liza thought that it was rude and forgot how aggressive and inappropriate Harry was when she met him. She also did not remember how loud he was until he yelled "Hey Liza" when he saw her. She was taken off guard and shivered when Harry Jr. yelled. Liza was mild-mannered and quiet, so she was put off by Harry. She told her mother that Harry's boisterous personality was obnoxious, but she was impressed with his self-confidence and hoped that a bit of that would rub off on her. She told her mother "I need to have more of a backbone. I mean this is only one date. I don't think there will be a second one. Maybe Harry's aggressiveness and self-confidence will affect me in a positive way. Liza's mom said "that's the way to look at it Liza". Liza's mom was well-acquainted with aggressive men. Liza's dad was very aggressive and rude. He did not feel well much of the time he and Liza's dad were married, and he took out his pain and pitty on Liza's mother. Liza and Liza's mom remembered Paul, the father who is now deceased, as someone who was always agitated by something. Liza's mother said "the sky could be a beautiful shade of blue and the grass a deep shade of green and your father would say how bright the sun was and how the weeds were taking over the yard. "Nothing could ever please that man." Liza replied "well mom I love you....you know that. But, you had nothing to do with the shade of the sky or the color of the grass. Liza's mom said "Yes, I know that. But, your Dad seemed to blame me for everything." "I'm sorry mom." said Liza. Liza's mom thought that her daughter was too introverted and standoffish so today she would encourage her to take a chance and accept the date with Harry Conover Jr. "It will be good for you Liza. You don't have to marry the boy." Liza's mother said. She continued, "No one is perfect Liza. Your father certainly was not, but I learned to adapt." Liza then said "I guess you can get used to anything if you do it long enough. Her mother said, "Well, I did!" After Liza ended her call with her mother, she decided that she would not cancel the date with Harry and hoped she would not regret the decision.

CHAPTER 13

JR. AND LIZA'S
FIRST DATE

It was the day of Liza and Harry Jr.'s date. Although she thought she did not care about how she looked, she nervously picked her favorite slacks and shirt. She fussed over her hair and wore perfume…a near first for Liza. After Harry picked up Liza for their date in the BMW he inherited from his father, he drove to the Italian restaurant in Dempsey. Liza thought that Harry drove like a cat out of hell. He had a lead foot and thought it was funny to weave in and out of traffic. At one point Liza told Harry to "slow down!" He commented "oh sorry sometimes I have to remind myself in this peppy car that I'm not on the German autobahn. Liza said "well recommendation there!" "Well, I am recommending you SLOW DOWN!" Liza exclaimed loudly. Liza felt like Harry was flaunting his wealth through his car (a BMW) and she did not like it one bit. As far as the date, Liza felt like it started off badly when Harry Jr. honked for her in front of her apartment instead of ringing or knocking on the door. It immediately put her in a foul mood. Consequently, Harry Jr. was pissed off because he thought Liza was a back seat driver. After Liza commented to Harry Jr. to slow it down, the conversation between the two shut down. Things in the car became a little icy between them. After arriving at the restaurant, Harry continued to exhibit his rudeness when he ordered wine without asking what kind Liza preferred, and he smacked his food when he ate. But again, Liza had very low self-esteem and felt good that someone asked her out even if he was a buffoon. The dinner was tasty although Harry complained to the waiter that the pasta was not "al dente" and the sauce lacked oregano. Liza rolled her eyes. After dinner, Harry belched loudly and exited to the bathroom without saying a word to Liza. After he left the table, Liza rolled her eyes and thought "what an idiot." At this point she said to herself "I will never go out with this man again! I mean this child again". When Harry returned from the restroom, he paid the bill, complained about the price and left a miniscule tip for the waiter. As Harry and Liza were getting back into Harry's car, Harry stumbled although he had only one glass of wine. He fell to the ground but picked himself up with the help of Liza's hand. He then used her hand to pull her onto the seat of the car. Spastically, he pulled Liza's arm in the direction of the back seat. He when ripped off her tights and skirt and proceeded to rape Liza. It was not consensual. It was rape. It was Harry's first sexual encounter although he was accused of rape in high school that was never proven. It was definitely Liza's first sexual experience. After the incident, Harry returned to the driver's seat and told Liza that she could excuse herself to the bathroom if needed. Liza was completely humiliated and frightened. Harry said nothing while he picked his teeth with a credit card. Liza sat in the passenger seat shocked and scared. She did not move and told Harry Jr. to take her home. After arriving at her apartment, Liza exited the car without saying anything. Harry Jr. said "see ya" and nothing about calling her again. So, Liza assumed that there would be no second date with Harry Jr. Quite frankly, she was fine with never seeing Harry again. Liza entered her apartment crying and called her mother immediately. Liza's mother told her she sounded upset. Liza told her mother that "she thought she was raped by Harry". Her mother said "what do you mean you think you were raped?" Liza explained that she and Harry had sex after dinner that was not consensual. "Sounds like rape to me." Liza's mother said. Then Liza explained the date to her mother "It was horrible mom…a real nightmare. Harry was so rude and treated me like dirt!" She continued and told her mother "Harry was completely terrible to me. He honked his horn to tell me he was at my apartment to pick me up, he belched the ABC's at dinner, forced me to have sex with him in his car and said nothing when he dropped me off at my apartment." Liza's mother said "That bastard!" Liza was happy that she and her mother had a candid discussion about premarital sex prior to her first experience. Her mother said "well Liza, you know that I would prefer that you not have sex until you are married, but I understand what happened to you was beyond your control." Liza said "yes, it was mother". Hopefully, Harry wore a condom." her mother said. Liza then lost her patience and said "how many rapists wear condoms mother?" Liza's mother said, "you raise a good point Liza, but watch yourself for any signs of disease or pregnancy." Liza said "God forbid that I would get pregnant by a complete imbecile on my first sexual encounter!" After the date with Harry, Liza waited for her period to show itself, but it never did. For her peace of mind, Liza tried to fabricate a date that her period was due but after several attempts of denial realized it was not going to happen. Liza had never wanted children. She never liked the way her mother was treated and how her father treated women. When she was a little girl she never played with dolls, never pretended to have a baby, or ever dreamed of raising a child. It just was not in her DNA. She never had a role model that convinced her that children were advantageous or that it was normal to get married or have a family and grow old with a husband. Liza's parents were not strong role models for Liza, and they did not have a particularly good marriage. Liza never admired their relationship as she grew up and never saw the advantages to having a family herself. She thought her father was an egotistical man with a huge chip on his shoulders, chronic health issues and depression. Her mother, who she loved very much, was not a positive role model as a mother. Although Liza admired her mother for the woman she was, she felt her mother was highly dependent on a man who treated her like shit and was drowning in his own depression. So, considering her assessment of "family life" that she experienced growing up, Liza thought she could do better without it. Regarding her sexuality, Liza had a "pie in the sky" attitude. She always thought she would be a virgin until she was married And, only have sex with a loving husband. Unfortunately, Harry Jr. Conovers ruined this for Liza, and she became very depressed. After laying on her bed and crying for a couple of days, Liza hoped out of the bed and said "it is time to make some decisions. She took a long shower and visualized washing the dirt off of her body that Harry Jr. left on her. After showering, Liza dried off and kicked the towel that she had dropped when drying herself off across the room. She felt almost elated that she was prepared to address the situation she found herself in. She thought "why can't I marry a man who would treat me nice and be kind to me?. I don't have to settle for a pervert rapist that can't control his dark fantasies. Why can't I marry someone who respects me and doesn't scare me? And, why can't I marry a man who believes that fidelity is the cornerstone to a healthy marriage? Am I looking for someone who is unobtainable? Liza said no, I am not. There is someone out there for me!" After having the internal conversation with herself, Liza decided that she would table the issue until she spoke further with Harry Jr. For the remainder of the day, Liza decided that she would focus on her upcoming graduation from Demsey U. She did not expect anyone from her side of the family to attend. Her father was on his deathbed, and she did not ask anyone else to attend. Instead, she focused on finalizing paperwork from her student loan to the University. She also would finish the dress she was making for graduation. Liza was quite accomplished in sewing and had made several workshirts for her father and a couple of dresses for her mother. After stewing in her thoughts for a few days and completing everything for her upcoming graduation, Liza called Harry one Sunday morning knowing that she had to be the first to contact him about the pregnancy since she never heard from him since the dinner and did not expect to hear from him. After dialing Harry's phone number, he finally answered on the fifth ring. He answered the phone in a fake British accent and Liza made the motion of gagging as she stuck her finger down her throat. Harry said in his cocky voice "oh hey Liza, what's up?" Liza told Harry that she had not had a period since their date and that she was concerned that she might be pregnant by Harry. Harry replied, "You might be what by who?" Liza was disgusted that he would take something so serious so frivolous. She them lost her temper and yelled "by you Harry, pregnant by you!" Harry asked Liza if she had taken a pregnancy test. Liza told Harry she had not taken a pregnancy test but that she was very regular and had never missed a period. Liza explained to Harry that since they had unprotected sex she grew concerned." Harry was flustered and told Liza "Well for god's sakes Liza before you get your panties in a wad, take a test!" Liza said "wow Harry. Spoken like a true linguist." Harry said "what is a linguist?" Liza said "never mind". Harry urged Liza to take a test and call him back with the news. After ending the call with Harry, Liza went to the store and bought a pregnancy test. She thought, "This cannot wait any longer". Back home alone and scared, Liza opened the pregnancy test, peed on the stick and waited for the results. Her world slowly closed in on her immediately as the small line on the test turned bright blue. She thought there is a couple out there who would be cheering each other and kissing passionately with these results. I am young and pregnant without a spouse, and I am scared. Liza's fear turned to panic at the thought of having a child with

Harry Jr.. Staring at the pregnancy stick for a while, it was like Liza thought she could will it to be negative. She shook the stick with hopes that if she turned it a bit it would read negative. No such luck. In fact, the blue line continued to get darker. She then threw the stick across the room and hit her cat who took off like a racecar. After soothing the scared animal, she picked up the phone and called Harry Conover to tell him the news. Liza thought "boy is he gonna be pissed!" Liza became very anxious because she had not spoken to Harry Jr. awhile. She thought "He doesn't even acknowledge that we had sex. So, I cannot imagine how this is going to go." Harry answered the phone, Liza told him who it was and he said "who?" Liza rolled her eyes expecting that Harry would show her no support. After telling Harry Jr. Conovers the news of the pregnancy, he said "ooh, wow, oh boy! how could that happen?" Liza was livid at his response and said, "Well, unprotected sex to start with Harry!" And Harry in his Harry like way said, "Are you sure it is mine?" Liza was pissed since she had never had sex prior to Harry. She said "You moron. I was a virgin before I was raped by you! Harry raised his voice and said "Rape is a strong word Liza. You better watch who you say this to." Liza yelled back "I didn't do anything Harry! You forced me to have sex with you on the seat of your car. Remember the blood? You cannot say that you forgot that terrible moment when you lost your ability to control yourself. Harry said "no, but I remember the dirt your shoes left on my leather seats. It took me hours to clean the car." Liza said "So sorry to get your stupid car dirty Harry, but I think we have a more pressing issue to discuss right now!" Harry stumbled over his words and said "let's not jump to conclusions Liza. I think we are letting our emotions overtake us." Liza then said "I want to throw up right now. But first, I want to pull your private part off and choke you with it." Harry reacted "Wow Liza there is no reason to get vile over this. It takes two to tango!" Liza, still angry at Harry, said "I wish it were only a dance Harry. I am going to have a child…

with you! We have a lot of decisions to make now." In response to Liza's comment to make some decisions about the pregnancy he said. "Well I vote that you get an abortion." Liza said "No way. My family and I are philosophically against abortion." Harry said "Well, I am not sure what you just said, but I think it was that your not voting for that option right? Liza said nothing but her face turned beat red with anger. Harry said "It is real safe now and it would prevent us from having our lives ruined forever." Liza said "I'm sorry that your life would be ruined by bringing a child into this world Harry as a result of your bad behavior. Please be an adult for at least once in your life. Take responsibility for your actions!" Then Liza took the phone away from her ear and flipped off the phone with her other hand. This is what Liza then told Harry Jr. "I think we should proceed with graduation to avoid any rumors of why we did not finish school. After graduation, I will go away and have the baby, and then we will take it from there." Then Harry said "You mean have the child alone? How will you do it by yourself?" Liza said "I am stronger than you give me credit. Quite frankly, I think the process will be easier if I just deal with it myself. At this point no one will know. I'll of course tell my mother but that will be it. You'll have to help me financially with travel and hospital bills and anything else I might need, but that should not be hard for you according to your past comments about your wealth." Harry stumbled over his words and said "well Liza I don't know what you think you know about any money. But, I want to save as much as possible. For my future of course." Liza then said "of course you do Harry, but I'll tell you that my entire savings will be wiped out after having this child. And, by the way, your future was decided when you threw me on the seat of your car and raped me. So, I think you can do your part!" Harry stammered around and meekly said "Well, what is my part Liza?" She said "As I said before, I will need help with transportation, hospital bills and any kind of baby care I will need while I am out of town." Harry said "Wow that can really add up." Harry Jr. had difficulty parting with his money but since Liza agreed to keep the pregnancy private as well as the rape accusation, he agreed to the monetary responsibility. Liza said to Harry Jr. "Out of site...out of mind." No one will suspect that anything has happened as long as we both keep our mouths shut. Harry, by this time, was turning green thinking about the expenses he would incur from the birth of the baby. Harry said "But Liza where will you go?" Liza said "I have done some research and have read that having babies in France is pretty low-key and inexpensive. Healthcare is free in France so medical costs should not be a big issue. There are three levels of maternity units in France. Level one is for normal births, and levels 2 and 3 are for moderate and urgent births. So, this reassures that my baby will get the most attention. Harry noticed that Liza referred to the baby as "her baby". He was jealous, and Liza did not care. So, my decision is made. I will have my child in Paris. I have never been there and if I am going to be in a situation that is not exactly pleasant, I want to do what I can to change the outcome. Liza thought that some distance away from Dempsey might diffuse the situation a bit. Plus she wanted to egg on Harry's jealousy a bit. Liza said. "No one will see me until I am back in Dempsey, and I have had the child. Liza continued...now, we have not talked about marriage Harry, but I think we should consider it to give my child a proper birth and name." After looking like he had seen a ghost, Harry responded "So I suppose you have nixed the abortion idea for sure right?" Liza's face turned two shades of dark red and she said "Harry, we have talked about this and I explained to you that I am against abortion. DID YOU NOT UNDERSTAND ME? Or, are you incredibly dense and have the world's thickest brain?" Harry replied, "well some people have said I am a little dense, but I prefer to call it *innocently curious.* For the thick brain thing, I am pretty sure that I have a large head with a huge brain". Liza said "whatever Mr. Big Brain innocently curious boy, have all your questions been answered?" He said yes they have. "Just one more final thing Liza It is the topic of marriage. We really don't know each other very well. Don't you think we should get to know each other first?" Liza said "No, I do not think we should get to know each other. I know what kind of person you are and frankly we have not been anointed with a lot of time here. You did not get to know me before you threw yourself on me without my consent. So, if you want me to keep my promise to not tell anybody about the rape, you will agree to give my child a name and support me through this pregnancy." Harry surprisingly had nothing to say to Liza's comments. The discussion was over. After she hung up the phone, Liza was proud of the strength she exhibited with Harry. "He will think twice before messing with me again." She thought. And, Liza was right. Harry was a little scared of Liza after this. Harry sent graduation announcements to everyone under the sun so he would get gifts. Liza did not care about the gifts. She was most excited about the freedom graduation would offer. She had always felt so awkward around her college classmates, and she had few friends. Harry did not care about the scholastic knowledge that he had acquired in college since he would inherit his mother and father's wealth. But now, with a child on the way, Harry Jr. was saddled with a new responsibility he never expected. At that point Harry Jr. became angry at the world. He was not angry that he did not resist a dark urge inside of him to rape Liza. And, he never faulted himself for the error he made. He simply viewed the situation as a test that he would have to deal with…that was sent to him by God. So this was Harry Jr.'s life. He had no friends or family that he could rely on. He knocked up a lonely unwanted woman that thought he was an idiot. Because of his family's wealth, he felt unencumbered to basically do anything. Though he did not expect his plans to include getting married and raising a child so early in his life…especially with someone like Liza. Harry had dreamed of settling down with a beautiful debutante, joining the local country club and spending his days doing exactly what he wanted…nothing! That dream was ruined after he raped Liza on his first date with her. Liza had always fantasized the potential for romance in Paris. Of course, she was not going to be there to meet the love of her life. But, she thought, "I am not opposed to the idea." So, that is what in part led to her decision to have the baby in Paris. Of course, all Harry could think of was the money it would take to have a baby in Paris, but Liza didn't care what Harry was thinking. Harry actually asked "Liza do you really think it is necessary to go all of the way to Paris." Liza quickly felt guilty about suggesting Paris but then responded to Harry. "Yes Harry I do think it is necessary to go out of the country to have the baby…the baby that I would not be having if it were not for you. It is the least you could agree to do. Remember, you are the reason I am pregnant." She reminded Harry that they were going to be graduating soon so the timing was good. Harry continued to be the asshole that he always seemed to be to Liza. During the pregnancy, he never asked her how she was feeling. He never wanted to talk about the child. And, he continued to pout about "Liza getting to go to Paris" to have the baby. The pregnancy reminded her of Harry's attack on her, and she lost interest in him completely. Harry Jr. did not understand Liza's reluctance to being close to him. But, she remained distant from him for their entire marriage. Anytime Harry would try to be intimate with Liza she would claim she was sick and push him away. Harry's attack on Liza turned her off to any interest in Harry and sex. He did not get it. "That was months ago…that was year's ago." Harry would say as if it was a 24-hour bug that she should get over." Unfortunately for Harry Jr,. his attack on Liza was an unforgivable assault with negative emotions that would last a lifetime. But, Liza would remind herself that the baby is Harry's child, and he will be in our life for a very long time. So, Liza said "I better sit back and accept the ride." The couple agreed that Liza would have the baby in Paris. Since she was in her third trimester, she would go immediately after graduation. No one in Dempsey would know that Liza was pregnant. Prior to her trip to Paris she stayed confined to her apartment and showed little of herself. She was rail thin and wore clothes that concealed the baby bump that was obvious to her but not so to other people. Liza would fly from New Orleans (Kenner, LA) about 65 miles away from Dempsey to New York where she had a layover enroute to Paris. She would stay overnight in New York, then fly to Paris' (Charles de Gaull Airport). Prior to her trip to Paris, Harry and Liza graduated. Liza graduated with honors. Harry barely graduated. The couple had no relatives attend graduation and it was simply another day to the two of them. Liza's mother and Harry were the only people who knew of the pregnancy. So, Harry Jr. and Liza's birth plan was set. The graduation was located at a dark and depressive concert venue in Dempsey. The ceremony was pretty uneventful other than Harry Jr. tripping as he walked across the stage in front of the graduation presenters. Liza swore that Harry Jr. tripped on purpose to get attention. Although, Harry Jr. claimed it was an accident. When he finally got up from the ground, Harry faced the crowd, gave a bow and said desole' meaning sorry in French. Liza said under her breath "what a doofus!" She was embarrassed for Harry Jr.. After graduation, Harry and Liza went to a local burger restaurant and ate lunch. They reminiscenced about the lazy days when life seemed so easy, no babies, no big decisions that had to be made. Liza was shocked at Harry Jr.'s apparent realistic gaze into the future of their life together. For the first time, Liza thought that Harry Jr. understood that their lives were not necessarily the fairy tale life that they had dreamt of as children. It touched her, although the feeling ceased quite quickly after he tried to belch the National Anthem and was extremely proud. After graduation and lunch, Liza returned to her apartment and began prepping for her European trip. Her plane trip was scheduled, her hotel was reserved and her temporary apartment in Paris was booked. She was leaving for Paris tomorrow the day after graduation. She packed her favorite books, asthma medicine, chex mix and the baby medallion that she privately wore on a chain around her neck. Although Liza never thought she wanted children, she became very emotional about the baby that was growing inside of her. She thought that this pregnancy was her opportunity to create something of her own. Something that she didn't have to share. Surprisingly, the pregnancy made her feel warm and happy.

CHAPTER 14

PARIS

T he next morning, Liza dropped her cat off at her friend
Catherine's apartment and then drove to New Orleans. Liza
insisted on going alone to the airport to expedite her freedom from Harry Jr. and Dempsey. Although she loved the town of
Dempsey when she first moved there, she learned to dislike it due to
the harsh memories of meeting Harry Jr., the rape, etc. The flight to
Paris had a layover at JFK airport in New York. She grabbed a bite to
eat and walked a little around the city until someone asked her for
money, and she felt threatened. Liza stayed in a moderately priced
hotel in New York near JFK. Harry did not approve. He thought the
hotel was beneath the Conovers' name. Liza did not care. After an
uneventful night, Liza boarded the plane to Paris. It would be an
approximate 7 hour and 46-minute flight. The flight was turbulent
and Liza was very nauseated. She drank 7-up and ate crackers the
entire flight to try and combat the nausea. It worked a little to help
Liza, but she still felt ill. During the flight to Paris, Liza's seat was located by a man who introduced himself as Stephen and talked about
his trip to Paris. Stephen explained to Liza that he was traveling for
business and told her that he was leaving his wife and child behind
in Chicago. Liza had a different reason for her trip to Paris, but, she
chose not to share the information with the man. She maintained

her pregnancy secret from a total stranger who could probably care less why she was there. Instead, Liza made up a story that she was visiting her sister who lived in Versailles, a city near Paris. Liza always dreamed of having a sister so this made-up story gave her the opportunity to fantasize whatever she wanted. She told the man that her sister was a very famous writer in Versailles and that she lives with her husband who is a copywrite attorney and her two children. She described her sister's children to the man. Alain, the oldest child of her sister, means little rock or handsome and Alcide, the youngest child means strength. She bragged about their beautiful home and how wealthy they were. "My sister, Anne, changed her name to Agnes which means pure or cleansed." Liza continued "You see all of her children's names are French. So she changed her name to something French as well." The man, who clearly looked like he wished he could be doing something...anything...less boring said. "I see. How interesting." After several boring hours on the plane, the pilot announced the imminent landing and asked that everyone prepare. The man sitting next to Liza was clearly excited about landing and the conversation between Liza and the man stopped. The two side-by-side passengers on the flight to Paris wished each other well and prepared to land. After landing at the airport, the man sitting by Liza rolled his eyes as he walked off of the plane. Liza took a shuttle to her hotel and checked into her room where she immediately fell asleep on her bed. The room was small, and she wished that she had booked a larger room in Paris. After contemplating requesting a larger room, she decided against the idea and continued to lie on the bed. She immediately fell asleep and dreamt about her recent graduation. It was a nightmare actually. In the dream, Liza was the Valedictorian of Dempsey U and was presenting a speech prior to the diplomas being handed out. As she was speaking to the graduates in the audience, a number of students carrying signs walked in the front of the graduate sitting area. The signs read "Knocked up Val

D. (referring to Liza the valedictorian). Everyone of the graduates started chanting "She's knocked up...she's knocked up!" Waking from the nightmare, Liza tried to shake off the dream with a hot shower. She patted her baby bump and said to the unborn child "Don't listen to those mean people. You are mine, and I will always take care of you." Liza surprised herself with the excitement that she felt about the new baby. "I have never felt this way about pregnancy before." Liza thought. Liza then made her way down to the gift shop. She wanted a travel guide for some sightseeing ideas. While in the hotel gift shop, Liza met a young woman who was visiting her sister in Toulouse, the Occitanie Region of France. It is a 6 ½ hour trip from Toulouse to Paris so the woman was staying at the hotel and enjoying a little Parisian culture. The girl, Maria, was around the same age as Liza and commented on Liza's pregnancy. Liza was an introvert and found Maria to be a little intrusive. But, Liza responded with a "hello". and Maria noticed the small baby bump that Liza carried underneath her oversized shirt. Although the bump was barely visible, Maria noticed perhaps because she was sensitive to the issue of pregnancy. Maria told Liza that she and her husband had been trying to conceive for some time but were having difficulty getting pregnant. The situation was very troubling for Maria who said that she and her husband desperately wanted a baby. She grew up in a large family and wanted a large family herself. She said that she had tried to adopt unsuccessfully, considered invitro fertiliza-tion but realized that it cost too much. Maria said that she and her husband have just lived with their despair. She told Liza that it is so upsetting to see so many homeless women in Paris that are pregnant. She continued and told Liza that many of the women have their ba-bies and leave them on the streets of Paris because they don't have the money to raise a child. And then, bing! A light bulb went off in Liza's brain. In order to shield my child from the reputation of being the child of an unwed mother, and save my reputation in Dempsey,

I could make up a story that I discovered an infant on the streets of Paris and brought her home with me. I would give Elizabeth a home in Dempsey and shield her from the rumors that she was the result of an unwanted pregnancy. In addition. I would look like an angel for doing so. I would tell Harry to keep his "big, fat" mouth shut and all of our friends in Dempsey would think that Elizabeth was a rescued child born on the streets of Paris. She said to herself "No one knows I am pregnant except my mother who I am sure would keep my secret safe." After saying goodbye to Maria, Liza returned to her room and took another nap. Pregnancy wiped Liza out. She was tired all of the time. This time during her nap she dreamt of being in a park with Elizabeth. Elizabeth swung while being pushed by Liza and then she was running around the park with an ice cream cone in her right hand. She hit a rock and took a fall. Liza ran and picked the little girl up and soothed her from the fall. Liza felt warm with emotion as she dreamt of the little girl. And again, she was surprised that she felt like she did about the little girl considering she thought she never really wanted a child. After waking up from the nap, Liza drank a large bottle of water and noticed that she was having contractions, her back was hurting, and she was having an urge to go to the bathroom…signs of labor. But, Liza rallied and seemed to find the energy to visit a local cafe for dinner. At the restaurant that was below the hotel, she ordered the Croque-monsieur that is basically a ham and cheese sandwich.

CHAPTER 15

LIZA'S WATER BREAKS/ HARRY JR. AND LIZA ARE MARRIED

A fter taking the last bite of her sandwich, Liza's water broke. She quickly called the restaurant attendant and informed the man what had happened. He quickly called for an ambulance that transported Liza to a local hospital. The birth of Elizabeth was quite normal and without any drama. The hospital staff was surprised that Liza was alone but asked no questions of her. Liza was very resilient and felt great after the birth of Elizabeth. She chose to hire a nanny for the first few weeks of Elizabeth's newborn life. This would give Liza the chance to rest and tour Paris while in France. During her trip. Liza visited the Eiffel Tower, went on a Bateaux Parisiens Seine River Gourmet Dinner and on a Sightseeing Cruise, she then attended a Paris Moulin-Rouge Cabaret Show with Champagne. Liza was having the time of her life and wondering how she would ever be able to marry a man like Harry Jr. But, she felt like she was in too deep at this point. During her trip to Paris, something wonderful happened. Liza, who never thought she would have a child fell in love with her newborn baby. She held Elizabeth tightly and told the baby that she was sorry she brought her into the world with a father like Harry Jr.. "I will keep you safe." Liza said and kissed Elizabeth on the lips. The child cooed. Liza told the newborn that she was sorry that she didn't have the willpower to leave Harry Jr. and that she was also sorry that her daughter's birth would be a lie forever. Elizabeth flashed her big blue eyes at her mother who reached down and told the little girl "I will never leave you." After Elizabeth was born, Liza returned to Dempsey and introduced Harry to Elizabeth. Harry held the little girl awkwardly and made awkward cooing noises that made Elizabeth cry. Liza would then retrieve the infant from Harry Jr. and the baby would stop crying. The couple agreed to be married after the child was born. It was not because they were in love, but because Liza thought the baby needed a traditional family situation. Harry did not want to get married, but Liza insisted and threatened Harry with the rape allegation. If he did not marry Liza, she would bust him for the rape. The couple knew that they were opposites with Harry Jr. being selfish, boisterous and almost impossible to love and Liza being quiet, kind and subdued. But, Liza, unlike Harry, felt that providing Elizabeth with a family, albeit emotionally crippled, was important. Liza already recognized the reality that her child had a few strikes against her before she was even born. She had a selfish, sexist father who was a disloyal and rotten man. Regardless, Liza was determined to make the marriage work solely for Elizabeth. Liza accepted the fact that her marriage would not be a day of bliss that she had dreamed of since she was a little girl. Instead, she was marrying a social buffoon who had knocked her up on their first date. Liza told her mother that her life did not turn out the way she had hoped. Her mother said that neither had her life. Regardless, when Liza returned from Paris, she and Harry planned their wedding. Well, actually Liza planned their wedding. Harry Jr. did very little. The ceremony included only Harry Jr. and Liza. This is how they wanted it. Liza hired a babysitter to look after Elizabeth during the ceremony. The couple opted out of a honeymoon. Instead, they drove from Dempsey to a nearby beach and spent a weekend with Elizabeth getting to know the young child. The wedding ceremony was very small with only the bride and groom present at the Justice of the Peace office in Dempsey. All of Liza's dreams of being a happy bride faded quickly as the "I-Do's" were said. It was not a romantic event but a stiff and structured procedure where the bride, groom said I do's reluctantly. There was no reception to honor the newly married couple, rather, the couple went home to see Elizabeth. Elizabeth was asleep when Harry Jr. and Liza returned home. She was a good sleeper and normally went to bed early and slept all night. Liza was the primary caretaker for Elizabeth. Harry Jr. did very little and complained when he had to do anything. "Why don't you help me more with Elizabeth?" Liza would ask Harry Jr. He would say "you are the mother; I am the father. It is called role delineation. Liza said "no it is not Harry Jr. It is called assholeism!" Harry Jr. said "what...oh yea I get it you are trying to be funny with all your mixed words and things." The conversation ended on that note. Liza showed Elizabeth around to all of her friends in Dempsey. Elizabeth was a beautiful little girl and learned how to walk, tie her shoes, and dress herself very early in her development. Harry would brag about her accomplishments as if he had something to do with her successes. He would say "that's my girl!" Harry would take Elizabeth around town to show her off. He carried the little girl like a trophy and held her awkwardly when showing the little girl off to his friends. If the little girl became snarky, Harry Jr. would run to his car, rush home and practically throw the little girl in the arms of her mother. All of the Conovers' friends who saw Elizabeth commented on her beauty and disposition. As Harry Jr. put Elizabeth on the ground his friends would say "look at that little girl, walking like a pro." Liza was a little more subdued about bragging on Elizabeth and would say, "she is a quick learner." As the years went by, Elizabeth proved to be a popular girl in Dempsey. She was a good student and a beautiful girl. Her standardized test scores were off-the-chart and her athletic skills as a gymnast were unprecedented. Elizabeth was also a very nice girl who befriended students who did not have many friends. She appreciated her place in life and understood that she was lucky. Other students liked her very much. During her years in high school, Elizabeth was the object of many boys' affection. But with all of her qualities, Elizabeth could be manipulative. She would bat her eyes and Harry Jr. would give her whatever she wanted. This caused many disagreements between Liza and Harry Jr. as Elizabeth's mother wanted her child to earn her way in life. Liza wanted her daughter to earn her own money for her car and Harry was not having it. Liza wanted Elizabeth to help out with school clothes, books, and other expenses. Harry Jr. would tell Liza "If we have the means to help our daughter out, how can you disagree with that?" This is when Harry Jr. began to be an intruder in his daughter's life. He would scrutinize the choices that Elizabeth would make, the clothes she would wear, and the boy's she would date. The daughter and father were close until she was in her late teens. When she went to college everything changed. She had spent some time choosing a college to apply. She finally chose Dempsey University to be close to her mother. Elizabeth did not want to leave her mother alone in the house with her father. Elizabeth would stay on campus and live in the same city as her parents. Over the next few years, her mother and father could barely stand each other. She had noticed a slow but steady deterioration of her parent's relationship, and it frightened her. Her father treated her mother like crap, and Elizabeth wanted to be there for her. Elizabeth stopped trying to suck up to her father to get what she wanted. She wanted to be her own person and choose her own path. She bought a used car that she had saved money from her job at a store in Dempsey. Her father did not like the fact that she seemed to be doing fine on her own. And, Elizabeth did not care.

Liza was proud of her daughter and often complimented her on her independence. Harry Jr. did not like Liza's comments. Harry Jr. wanted people to feel indebted to him. Liza would tell Harry Jr. to "let Elizabeth make decisions on her own!" Harry would come back with a "you leave it alone Liza". No one in the marriage seemed to give an inch. The conversations were always too loud and way too long. And, no conclusions were ever made. Harry Jr. normally stayed outside during the day so Liza rarely saw him. It was finally time for registration at Dempsey U. Elizabeth and her mother had shopped for Elizabeth's college clothes, and she decided to go through sorority rush. Although her mother wasn't thrilled about Elizabeth's interest in a sorority, Harry Jr. liked the idea of his daughter's interest in the Greek world. He felt like it was Elizabeth's way into society and thought she would attract a wealthy group of friends and marry up in the world. Elizabeth had always been proficient in tumbling and had taken gymnastics classes throughout her childhood. She had cheered every year in elementary, junior high and high school. She had also qualified for the Jr. Olympics and earned an award when she went. She decided that it was a natural move to try out for cheerleader for Dempsey's college football team. So, when the tryouts came around, Elizabeth decided to give it a shot and she was chosen as a cheerleader for the Dempsey University Bruins football team.

CHAPTER 16

ELIZABETH STARTS COLLEGE

Elizabeth started her freshman year at Dempsey University. She pledged a sorority, moved into the sorority house and made many friends. Although she did not see her mother or father as frequently as she did when she lived with them, she saw her mother frequently and her father less. Elizabeth's social schedule was intense as well as her academic schedule. One day she was walking to her class in the Science Department hallway and saw a boy that was standing by one of the classrooms waiting for his class to start. She passed by the boy and said hello. To her, he was the perfect man. Groomed, fit and handsome. He said hello and they looked at each other for a while. His name was John and he asked Elizabeth her name. John said that she looked familiar to him. She then explained that she was a cheerleader and John Moss told her he was a football player on the Dempsey U. football team. John said that "they must share a practice field." Elizabeth responded "We must because I think I have seen you on the field." They reciprocated how nice it was to meet each other and both walked away. There was an obvious attraction between the two, and they would meet again. When Liza's mother turned 80 years old, she was asked if she wanted to live with Harry and Liza by Liza not Harry Jr. who never liked Martha. Martha had lived on her own for several years after her husband had died. Although undiagnosed, Martha started showing signs of Alzheimer's that alarmed Liza. The conversation that Harry Jr. and Liza had about Martha was not friendly. It was a contentious discussion when discussing Martha and her living situation. Harry did not want Martha to live with them. He thought that Martha would cramp his style and monitor his activities that would be reported back to Liza. Liza assured Harry that Martha would not reign on his parade and that her living with them would be easier than Liza having to travel often to take care of her mother. Harry relented and finally agreed that Martha could live with them. Although Martha hated Harry, she decided that she would move in with Harry and Liza so she could watch him. Also, Martha's age and mental challenges were such that she felt like she needed protection...even if it was from Harry. Harry was consumed with Martha's money. She had a lot of money that she had accumulated over she and her husband's lifetime. Liza was the executor of Martha's will, and Martha had notated in her will that Harry should receive nothing from her inheritance. The rift between Martha and Harry Jr. caused a lot of conflict in the Conovers family. After Liza's dad had passed her mother had taken some of the stocks they had purchased and made a fortune from her investments. Martha proved to be a smart investor, and Harry Jr. hated it.

CHAPTER 17

LIZA'S MOTHER MOVES IN

O ver the years since Martha had known Harry, he had developed an aggressive and threatening personality. He was a paranoid and angry man who had dealt with his internal demons since birth. He thought Martha was nosy and tried to interfere in his and Liza's life. Harry was suspicious of Liza's mother because she had seen a young women Harry brought to his house when Liza was out of town. Martha had heard Harry having sex with many young girls in his bedroom, but she never told Liza because she did not want to hurt her daughter. Little did she know but that her daughter knew all about Harry's affairs. She simply did not care. Harry was afraid Martha would blab his secret to Liza. So, Harry told the old woman that the young girls she saw at his house only wanted to take a dip in the pool. Martha was, however, keen to Harry's extramarital sexual proclivities. Liza's mother knew Harry was not faithful to Liza, but she was scared of him. She also had cognitive and balance deficits from a stroke she had a couple of years back that made her paranoid. One time Martha told Harry that she knew what he was doing when Liza was gone. She mentioned hearing the voice of a young girl by the pool. Harry threatened

Martha, and then told her that the young girl she heard by the pool just wanted to go for a swim. He told her that the girl was a friend of Elizabeth's. Martha told her home health nurse about the conversation that she and Harry had regarding the female voice that Martha had heard by the pool. "Harry told me that he would hurt me if I told anyone." Martha told her home health nurse. The nurse said "I will not hesitate to tell my supervisor about his threat." She continued "If you would like for me to talk to Harry I will." Martha started crying and thanked the nurse for her offer. She said, "I will tell you if this happens again. We will wait and see." Martha finished. The young girl continued to call Harry and visited him often at he and Liza's home. One afternoon, the young girl was swimming with Harry and was hit in the head with a chair Harry had thrown into the pool. Intoxicated, Harry drove the young girl to a hospital outside of Dempsey and left the girl at the emergency entrance. To avoid a scandal, he did not want to take her to the local hospital. So, he drove further to another hospital in a city outside of Dempsey. When there, Harry put a note in the young girl's shirt pocket that she had been hit in the head accidentally with a chair. While drinking, Harry started acting like a three-year old and was throwing pool furniture into the pool. He thought it was funny. The young girl happened to be in his way and was hit in the head with the pool chair. After the accident, Harry placed a band aid over the bleeding gash on the young girl's head. Harry left her at the hospital alone without providing them with any detail information like a contact number or where she lived. Harry panicked and did not want Liza to find out about the young girl. Luckily for Harry, no one found out about the accident and the girl recovered with a bad headache. Elizabeth knew the girl and found out about the accident from another sorority sister. She asked her father to stop pursuing girls that she knew and her father said he was simply "young at heart." Elizabeth said to herself "you mean horny at heart! Every Sunday, the Conovers, Martha and the

Moss's went to lunch. On one particular Sunday the group dined at a local cafeteria that Harry Jr. and Liza often visited. After arriving back at Harry and Liza's house from lunch, Martha took a fall down the Conovers' stairs. She hit her head and died instantly. A rumor had circulated around Dempsey that Harry was responsible for Martha's fall, but nothing was proven. Harry never spoke of the incident with Liza although she always suspected that Harry had pushed her mother down the stairs. After Martha's death, Liza Conover received a significant amount of money from her mother. Liza's mother specified in her will that the money should be entirely gifted to Liza and not Harry. Further, she wrote a note to Harry that he saw after her death. The letter read, "I know what you did. I know what you do. Shame on you." Harry called her a bitch and Liza wondered what Martha knew about Harry. Although the money was entirely left to Liza, Harry knew that the money would be shared with him. Since Harry was influential in Dempsey and friends with the local police department, he was not considered a suspect in Martha's death.

CHAPTER 18

THE AFFAIR ON THE BOWLING LEAGUE

Martha's fall was determined an accident. One of the girls that Harry was involved with was on his bowling league. Her name was Honey. Honey was completely unlike the polished girls that Harry Jr. regularly sought after. She was a hairdresser in Dempsey; uneducated, unsophisticated and the town slut. Harry was not the only man in Dempsey who had slept with Honey. She had slept with the mayor of the town, the city commissioner and the head of the fire department. All of the men were married. Honey preferred married men. She thought they were more fun to chase. Although she thought most of them were in love with her, they were simply using her for sex. Honey was overconfident and delusional. None of the men loved Honey. They were sexually hungry and Honey made herself available to them. Although not beautiful, Honey was cute, voluptuous and outgoing. She was a big girl and poured herself into clothes that were too small to try and make herself look younger and fit. She wore her shoulder length hair in braids and frequently wore a ballcap to hide her not so recent highlight job. In Dempsey, Honey was considered white trash in the community and lived outside the city limits of Dempsey with her husband Warren. Liza knew there was someone on Harry's bowling team that he was sleeping with. Liza just did not know who it was. Although she knew Honey as the town sleaze bag, she never thought, in a million years, that Harry would involve himself with someone like her. Harry Jr. was too conscious of what other people thought of him to start a scandal. After Honey and her husband moved into an apartment within a few miles of the Conovers, Liza became a little more suspicious of Honey due to the rumors in town that Harry was seeing her. Honey was now living in "Liza's Dempsey," and she was not welcomed! Liza and Harry got into a terrible argument regarding Honey's move close to their house. She was convinced Harry planned it all so that he could sleep with Honey more often. "I know you had something to do with that slut's move by my house" said Liza. Harry responded "Liza, how stupid do you think I am to arrange something so bizarre?" Liza asked "Is that a rhetorical question Harry?" On occasion when they did run into each other...or when Honey was shopping at an expensive shop in Dempsey, the ladies would ignore each other and then shoot each other the bird behind each other's back. Then they would both rail against Harry for his stupidity. Although Harry despised conflict of any kind, he felt proud that he had two women who he felt were vying for his attention. Liza knew Harry was secretly patting himself on the back for nabbing two women who would share his bed, and she was humiliated. Although married for over 50 years, Liza shared a totally inactive sex life with Harry. They had not had sex for years, and Liza could not imagine herself ever having sex with Harry again. She was totally turned off by his indiscretions. When Liza brought up Honey to Harry, he would simply play ignorant and tell Liza he did not know who she was talking about. Conversely, he would reassure Honey that there was no love between he and Liza. That kept Honey, the clueless air head, satisfied for the time being. Liza simply did not care. She had given up on her marriage to

Harry Jr. years ago. She hated him for his unfaithfulness to her and had threatened to leave him a number of times in their relationship. But, Harry Jr. would beg her not to leave and buy her a nice gift. One time she threatened to leave Harry, and he bought her a new Lexus. Another time, he purchased a condo in Florida where she visited once. He had adopted the condominium as his sexual hideaway from Liza. She did not care. In fact, she helped him pack for his trip often.

CHAPTER 19

HONEY AND WARREN MCGRAW

oney and Warren met at a bar in Dempsey. Their first date included a slow dance, seven shots of whiskey and a romp in the sack. After a month of dating and a pregnancy scare, Warren proposed, Honey accepted and they were married a month later. Both uneducated, the McGraws barely survived on the low bartender salary Warren made and the minimum wage plus tips that Honey took in from her job as a hairdresser. Their appetite for buying things exceeded their paychecks and they always fought about money...the money they did not have. They lived on credit cards...high interest credit cards...and they were always in debt. Each blamed the other, but regardless of whose fault it was, they were in a marriage made in hell with a total lack of respect for each other. Both were serial enablers who served to totally screw up each other's lives. Unfortunately, neither would learn the hard lessons that accompany the responsibilities of growing up. This situation would serve to haunt them both throughout their lifetimes. Honey was not close to her parents and were happy that they lived in North Louisiana away from her. Her dad worked in the oil fields and her mother worked as a hairdresser. Honey's parents were strange people. Her dad, Joe, acted like he knew everything. He did not. Joe was a serial interrupter and frequently pissed people off who were around him. Honey's mother blended into the woodwork and always deferred to Joe as the expert about everything. They drove Honey nuts and she would make a scene anytime they were visiting she and Warren. Joe and Diane, Honey's mother and father argued about as much as Honey and Warren. Arguing seemed to run in the family. Although the fights between Honey and Warren were primarily about money, Warren always had his suspensions about Honey's fidelity. Although money would emerge as the cause of the arguments, Warren was actually pissed about the sexual rumors that circulated in the town about Honey. Warren had seen Honey talking to other men in town as he drove to his job. When asked about the encounters with other men, Honey would always claim that the conversations were casual, and she would change the subject. Still, there was an air of suspicions that floated over Honey and Warren's relationship. Over the years, Warren began to lose faith in Honey. He lost faith in her loyalty and trustworthiness. She never kept her promises and Warren started getting more suspicious as Harry had entered the picture. Sex with Honey was infrequent and small acts of kindness like a nice dinner or a sweet card were nonexistent. Honey had become vulgar and unkempt. She had smoked since Warren had first met her, but the habit started to get on Warren's nerves. She left her cigarette butts in the toilet and failed to brush her teeth at night or take a bath regularly. Warren would bring the behavior to her attention, and she would become enraged and spout out everything she didn't like about Warren. Honey would yell at Warren and tell him "You have bad breath and you smack when you eat!" This was Honey's strategy to keep him down. The McGraws were stuck! They were stuck in a world of apathy and no personal accountability. They blamed everyone else for their irresponsibility and were so mired in their own depression that they failed to embrace any personal accountability for the problems in life. At the beginning of the marriage, Honey and Warren fought, made mad love, and fought again. The bedroom was the only place they felt compatible and eventually that eroded too. Without their passion in the bedroom, they were simply roommates. As Warren started working nights, he gave Honey the gift of time. She had time for her affair with Harry Jr. Conovers. Warren noticed the distance Honey formed when she was seeing Harry, but he just thought she was working a lot of hours and tired. A rage burned inside of Warren's heart as he recalled the number of Dempsey friends who had said that Honey was screwing around on him. He did not want to believe the rumors, but they were becoming too vast to ignore. Honey and Warren had lost a child. In fact, Honey had miscarried at least three times creating resentment between she and Warren. They wanted a child but knew that they should not be parents. Parents have to be responsible caretakers of vulnerable little people. Their selfishness would not have been appropriate to have a child. So perhaps the stars were aligned that they were unable to have children.

CHAPTER 20

HONEY AND HARRY JR.

Honey and Harry's relationship was entirely based on sex. They had nothing in common and did not hold fond feelings for each other. They were both simply unhappy married people who lacked the emotions involved in being a faithful partner. They understood each other and both wanted the same thing...sex...and only sex. The excitement resided in the secret. The secret that Honey and Harry Jr. shared about being together. They thought no one knew their secret, but the little hand pats and innuendos that were exchanged on the bowling league were noticed by the members on the team. And, the members of Harry's bowling team were more than happy to share the information with people who lived in Dempsey. So, what Harry and Honey considered a secret between the two was a well-known fact among many residents in Dempsey. About two months into their relationship, Harry invited Honey to his condo on the Florida coast. Liza was at a Junior League conference in Tennessee. Honey said she had to work at first but asked someone to fill in so she was able to go with Harry. They would leave on Friday and return on Sunday before Liza arrived home. As they drove to the coast, they exchanged a bit of pleasantries and flirted aggressively with each other in the vehicle. Honey knew not to pressure Harry Jr. in any way with questions like "Do you love me?" and "Do you think about me?" although she always had a slim hope that the answer would be yes. She knew it would not be yes and did not want to hear the answer. As they entered the condominium complex Harry asked Honey if she was hungry. She said, "for food?" He laughed and said "yes." Honey said she was hungry, and Harry mentioned that he had made reservations at his favorite seafood restaurant on the coast. Harry continued and said, "I have a couple of friends in the complex that I'd like to invite. Do you mind? Honey said no, and Harry called his friends and gave them a place and time for dinner. As Harry and Honey entered the condo, they had a quickie and took a shower together to get ready for dinner. The restaurant was in walking distant from the condo, so they walked. Honey asked about his friends and Harry said he had known them since he purchased the condominium. He failed to tell Honey, however, that his friends were young pretty women whom he had sex with in the past. Upon entering the restaurant, Harry acknowledged the women who had arrived early for dinner. They were already tipsy from the wine they consumed before Harry and Honey had arrived. As Harry arrived at the women's table he said "well, it looks like you guys are having fun." Honey's biggest nightmare was about to come true. The two women were volup-tuous and scantily clothed. They were much more attractive than her, and she was angry that Harry had invited the women. After the introductions and ordering dinner, Harry asked the girls what they were doing that night. One girl said, "hanging out with you Harry like we always do." Harry was uncomfortable but said "okay." Honey kicked Harry under the table, and he said "Ow!" "What an idiot!" Honey thought. So, after dinner the girls decided to meet Harry and Honey at the condo for a nightcap. During the entire walk back to the condominium, Honey was scolding Harry for what she said was a total "shit show." Honey did not know what the girls expected but she assumed it wasn't a bedtime story. She felt confident that it was Harry wanting sex from all three girls. Upon arriving back at the condo, Honey started chugging tequila. The girls were already intoxicated but also started drinking shots of tequila. The drunker the girls got the more clothes they started shedding. Although Honey was uncomfortable, she started shedding her clothes too. Thanks to the tequila Honey lost her inhibitions. Good thing since the girls in the nude were much more attractive than Honey. Harry was just being a sleazy voyeur. He knew if the night continued to progress as it was currently progressing then he would get very lucky. And the night did progress. Both girls and Honey had their clothes off and started to undress Harry who appeared to be paralyzed with excitement. The night continued with sex between the three of them. After they were finished, the girls took off and Honey and Harry fell asleep without talking. Upon awakening, Honey served Harry with a serious attitude about the prior night and the sex with the girls. "I cannot believe that you thought that was okay" said Honey. "Well, you didn't seem too offended by the situation Honey." said Harry. "Well, I was!" said Honey. She continued, "Why would you think that I was into that Harry? continued Honey. Harry said, "You have always seemed to me to be sexually open Honey. Are you not?" he continued. Honey said, "No one is as sexually open as you Harry so I do not know how you can judge." Harry chuckled and walked toward Honey. After grabbing Honey, he pushed her onto the bed and tried to get intimate with her. She brushed him off and said she was mad at him. He shrugged and said he was going to get some sunscreen. When he returned from the store Honey was naked in the bed and told Harry she was sorry. Harry jumped on her and said everything was A-okay. After having sex, Harry and Honey ordered a pizza and opened a couple bottles of wine. Honey was a beer person but she thought she should act like she liked wine with Harry. She

actually hated it. After eating the pizza, Harry and Honey, intoxicated, went to sleep. The next morning they were scheduled to leave
the condo and head back to Dempsey. Both of them had lied to their
mates. Liza was at a conference in north Louisiana. Harry Jr. had
told Liza he was going golfing alone in Florida. Honey told Warren
that she was going to a conference about coloring hair. Warren did
not care. Neither did Liza. Warren did not know about Harry and
Honey. Although, one time he was behind them in the drive-through
line at a local fast-food restaurant. He thought that the girl in the
car in front of him looked like Honey, but he thought "No way.
Honey is at home tonight." Honey was lucky. The drive-through
service was uncharacteristically fast this night. Liza started getting
suspicious of the smell Honey left on Harry's clothes. Harry did not
smoke, but Honey did smoke and it permeated Harry's clothes. He
would simply blame the smoke on his friend Albert. Harry knew that
Albert would play his game and keep his mouth shut about Harry's
affair with Honey. Albert was a longtime friend of Harry's. They
had known each other since elementary school. Albert was one of
the only kids in Harry's elementary school who did not make fun
of him. For this, Albert received Harry's utmost dedication. When
Liza would ask Harry about the smell on his clothes, he would say
that "he had lunch with Albert, and he was smoking. Liza had no
reason to not believe Harry. She and Harry had dined with Albert
and his wife many times.

CHAPTER 21

ELIZABETH AND JOHN MOSS

The conversation between Honey and Harry Jr. turned to Elizabeth when they were in Florida. Honey was not particularly interested in hearing about Harry Jr.'s family. Honey was jealous of Harry Jr.'s family although her intense jealousy of his family generated interest in a nosy kind of way. Harry Jr. told Honey he was proud of Elizabeth and her talent as a cheerleader at the local college in Dempsey. He mentioned her marriage to John Moss a 6 foot sandy-blonde quarterback at the College in Dempsey. But he did not elaborate on John's accomplishments. John majored in criminal justice and Elizabeth fashion merchandise. Elizabeth was the only child of Harry and Liza Conover. Elizabeth had been a cheerleader since elementary school and was a local dance instructor for a number of years. She was a beautiful girl, but Elizabeth could be shallow and superficial. Responsibility can be given to Harry Conovers Jr. for these traits. He always told Elizabeth "it is your world, not anyone else's." She relied on her mother to remind her that she was a lucky girl and was very fortunate unlike many other people. John Moss, Elizabeth's husband, was from a close-knit family in Dempsey. His family had lived in Dempsey for decades. John's mother and father were parents who were "all in" their children's lives. They raised their children to be respectable and honest. John and his sister Ester lived a typical life in Dempsey. Close in age, they played barefoot in the Louisiana grass and caught lightening bugs on dark nights. Their parents frequently hosted crawfish boils in their backyard while Ester and John threw the football and played on the slip-n-slide. John's mother and father met at the electric company where they worked for 30+ years. John's father was an executive in the Dempsey office while his mother worked in accounts payable. Subsequently, they were engaged, married and became the parents of two children, John and Ester. Ester was quiet and enjoyed cooking and crafts. John was a peculiar child. He was outgoing but had a temper as a young boy and would frequently get in fights with the boys at his school. He loved all sports especially football and he excelled at the game. He also played baseball and tennis at the local rec center from the age he could lift a ball. John and Ester were alike in that they both loved their family and each other very much. Ester liked to read and cook. Like John, she loved her mother and father very much. As John grew up, he became an accomplished football player. He played football in elementary and high school and won many trophies for his accomplishments. As John reached college age, he was recruited by the local University for the football team. He received a scholarship to play college football and his parents were pleased to defer the cost of college to the scholarship money. John's exceptional football ability drove a ton of Dempsey residents to the home games on Saturday night. The stadium roared with excitement and you could hear the noise from several miles away. College football was popular in the south. John's father had played football and his father as well. It was a tradition in John's family. When his family would get together they would pass around family photos of football highlights. John became somewhat of a celebrity in Dempsey as a college football star. Most of the town's people would be at the home games on Saturday night cheering on John and his team. Avid football fans would travel to out-of-state games to see John play. During one of his stellar performances as quarterback, a professional recruiter for the NFL attended one of his games. The recruiter became interested in John's as a quarterback. He spoke briefly with John after a game when John threw three touchdown passes. It was an exemplary game for John. Of course, he was elated. It was a dream of his to play professional football, and he finally saw the situation as an opportunity that could make his dream happen. Although John struggled to maintain a grade point average required to play college football, he was tutored in subject matters that he was failing in and ended up pulling his grades up to make him eligible to play football. He struggled a lot in school that never came easy for him. School was never a priority for John because he depended on getting a football contract and never thought that he would need an education. John's mother and father were a little more lovingly realistic about John's career path. Although John had a plan to pursue law if lllhe did not get an NFL contract, his parents were skeptical of his ability to get into a good law school. They felt like he did not have the discipline or stamina to pursue a law degree. They would gently discourage the law school aspiration, but John would not listen to their objections. He thought he would have no problem getting into a good law school. John was delusional. He liked the image of being an attorney more than the thought of working to become an attorney. Frankly, John lacked the brains for law. He was simply over his head with his thoughts of being an attorney and overconfident in his ability. John and Elizabeth first met when John tripped over Elizabeth on the football field. She was a college cheerleader. He knocked the cheerleader down during a game. She picked herself up and yelled in her soupy Louisiana accent "What is the deal. Are you blind?" John replied back "Screw you!" Elizabeth thought "boy he is cute." But the **SCREW YOU! REALLY?** After the football game, Elizabeth went to a fraternity party that a friend had invited her to. John was there. He was a member of the fraternity where the party was held. Elizabeth acted like she did not see him, but of course she did. As the two walked past each other, both acted as if they did not notice each other. John circled the room a second time and saw Elizabeth. She had blonde hair and long, dark, muscular legs. John liked what he saw. As he passed by Elizabeth he said, "funny running into you…again". She said "ha, ha". He apologized and asked if anything was strained, broken, etc. Elizabeth said no. But I could have lived without the "screw you" comment. He said sorry and could he get her a drink. She said yes and got a chill down her spine as she gazed at his broad shoulders. After complimenting John on his excellent game play. Elizabeth flashed John with her brilliant white smile and in her best Louisiana accent said "Go Bruins!" After random chit chat and several drinks later, John escorted Elizabeth upstairs to the game room. They were both feeling a little buzzed. As they both fell on the couch in the game room. Elizabeth said "oh, excuse me." John kissed her deeply. The two beautiful people made out all night on the game room couch in John's fraternity house. Waking in the early hours of the morning, John and Elizabeth both checked their phones for any calls and headed to the parking lot of the fraternity house. Elizabeth headed to her powder pink VW convertible. She sat in the driver's seat and motioned for John to get in the passenger side. As John sat in the passenger's seat, Elizabeth put her hand on his crotch and said,"nice to meet you". They both laughed and John gave Elizabeth a long and passionate goodbye kiss. Elizabeth drove to her sorority house. As she walked up the stairs to her room, a flurry of her sorority sisters stopped her to ask about John. Well, who is he? One person asked Elizabeth "Did you do it with him." Another asked "Is he a good kisser." Elizabeth replied "he is a divine kisser and no to the other question." And Elizabeth squealed, "he wants to be a professional football player or a lawyer whatever happens first" said Elizabeth in her southern accent. All of the girls laughed and said "good job Liz!" Liz continued "I don't care what he majors in as long as he makes a lot of money" she continued "Honestly, I just want to get married and have babies". Is that so awful?" she asked. "Of course not" her friends said in unison. She continued "don't we all just want that?" said Elizabeth as she tugged at her bra that had snapped in the back earlier. Elizabeth was beautiful but not the sharpest tool in the shed. What she lacked intellectually though she made up with pure sexual attractiveness. John called Elizabeth the next day reeling from the night before when he could not believe that someone so beautiful could like him. Elizabeth, this is John. She said "who jokingly of course but she knew who it was. Elizabeth was overcome with happiness that John called her. "I am so happy that you called" she said. John replied, "Did you honestly think I would not?" Elizabeth shrugged the question off. During the call John asked Elizabeth if she would have dinner with him at the fraternity house on Friday night. She quickly said "yes" and fist bumped the air. She was happy and could hardly wait to kiss John again. Although Liz had dated since she was sixteen, she never felt the passion for anyone like John. He fit every category that she envisioned from a boyfriend. He was sexy, handsome, a good athlete, potentially wealthy, a good kisser... and that was the depth of Liz's list. Although both slightly hungover from the Thursday night Exchange (Fraternity/Sorority party) both John and Elizabeth rallied to prepare for the second night of seeing each other. Elizabeth decided to shop for something to wear to the fraternity dinner. She thought "I need something that says I wonder what's under that sundress." She wanted a sexy outfit that would entice John. Elizabeth bought a yellow sundress with a red daisy print. The dress perfectly accentuated her figure and screamed "available and ready", and she was. John borrowed a polo shirt from his roommate and took a shower. That was the extent of his preparing for the date with Elizabeth. As Elizabeth carefully laid out her sundress on her bed she recited how the night would go with her roommate. "First we will have dinner and he will introduce me to all of his brothers. Then he will take me by the hand and walk me to my car and kiss me goodnight. Well, the first part of that scenario was correct. John introduced her to his fraternity brothers and they had dinner. Most of the fraternity brothers knew Elizabeth either romantically or as friends. And most of her sorority sisters had dated many of the fraternity members. After a dinner of Salisbury Steak, mashed potatoes and cherry cobbler for desert John walked Elizabeth to her car and pushed her into the backseat where he pulled the sundress off of her. So much for romance Elizabeth thought. She was hoping that the night would be unforgettable with manners and romantic overtones. But, she was completely infatuated with John so she did not care that the romance wasn't there. Her post fraternity dinner date with John was filled with apprehension and worry as Elizabeth wasn't on any form of birth control and had unprotected sex with John. He simply did not care. Elizabeth started counting backwards to her last period and then she started to really worry. "John she said, we didn't use any birth control. No, we did not." John said flippantly. Elizabeth drove back to her sorority house crying all of the way. She was pretty concerned with John's attitude toward no birth control. She thought it was irresponsible and risky. Elizabeth was angry at herself because she did care about birth control and knew that her behavior was irresponsible. "How could I be so stupid? Please don't let me be pregnant, please don't let me be pregnant!" Elizabeth screamed! After that, she pulled it together and exited her car. Rushing back to her room in the sorority house Elizabeth hit a patch of bumpy pavement and fell to the ground. Embarrassed, she looked around to make sure no one saw her, she wiped the loose dirt and gravel off of her opaque stockings and straightened her skirt. As she ran up the stairs to her bedroom she met her sorority sister, Laurie, on the stairs. Laurie saw the hole in her stockings and said,

"Girl, did you take a tumble?" Elizabeth rolled her eyes and said, "Yes I did Laurie. Thank you for noticing." Embarrassed by her clumsy behavior, Elizabeth rushed into her room and fell on her bed. She rubbed her knee that was bleeding from the fall and wiped it clean with antiseptic and a Band-Aid. After laying there for a bit, Elizabeth looked over at her side table where her phone sat and noticed the message light was blinking. By this time, Elizabeth's roommate. Laurie, Elizabeth's roommate, had entered the room and asked Elizabeth about her night with John at the fraternity house. She told Laurie that the dinner was terrible and that she had unprotected sex with John. Laurie hugged Elizabeth and said "Don't worry. I have had unprotected sex a number of times, and I have never gotten pregnant." Elizabeth did not feel much better because Laurie had a reputation of being a slut. Elizabeth yelled "It is time to drop the worry and plan the party!" "What's on the schedule Laurie? We need a party plan for Saturday night!" said Elizabeth. Laurie replied, "There is this awesome band playing at the "Gruber" tonight. *The Gruber was a local bar that was popular with the college crowd.* Just after Laurie mentioned the Gruber John called Elizabeth. "Hey Liz, this is John. What are you doing tonight?" John asked. Elizabeth explained that Laurie had mentioned a band that was playing at the Gruber. He said to Elizabeth that he knew someone in that band. He is on the football team. I will be there. Elizabeth was excited that she would see John again. Elizabeth said, "Well I guess I will see you there. John said "yes, you will". Although Elizabeth was still worried that she was knocked up, she was excited to see John again. Laurie and Elizabeth ate dinner at the sorority house and then took off in Laurie's BMW. Laurie's parents were rich. Elizabeth liked rich people. As Laurie and Elizabeth walked into the Gruber, John was singing with the band. He knew the guitar player and was called up to sing a number from Jimmy Buffett. After the song John made eye contact with Elizabeth and left the stage to talk to her. Then, the talking led to dancing, the dancing led to shot drinks, the shot drinks led to kissing, and the kissing led to sex in the bathroom. And again, Elizabeth had unprotected sex. She could not believe that she let herself do it again. She and Laurie returned to their room drunk and tired. Elizabeth passed out on her bed and dreamed that she was pregnant and unhappy. Her mood turned to relief when she realized it was a dream. Elizabeth woke up to a phone call from John asking if she wanted to have lunch in the park. She said, "Of course. I'd love to have a picnic in the park!" John said "good, but it isn't a picnic." He told Elizabeth that he would pick her up at noon. John picked Liz up in his Jeep Cherokee and they kissed immediately. They arrived at the park and laid their blanket out in a space near the bathrooms. Another couple was nearby on a blanket. They were both reading and attempting to be intimate, but when the man kissed the woman she screamed "no teeth". That pretty much broke the silence for Elizabeth and John who started laughing at the couple. Since John and Elizabeth had classes on Monday morning, they ended the picnic on Sunday early and returned to their houses. Both John and Elizabeth were seniors in college. They were scheduled to graduate in the fall. Based on what happened later with John, Elizabeth had no plans to get a job. She felt confident that her parents would help her out financially. John's future plans included getting drafted by the NFL and playing professional football for as long as he could. Elizabeth's aspirations included marrying someone with money. and marrying someone who would take care of her. John was cute she thought, but he was not marriage material. She knew that John's plans did not include getting married to a debutante of her caliber and taking care of her for life. The couple were clearly not reading from the same playbook. It was a fling between two college kids both agreed. They had no idea what their future had in store for them.

CHAPTER 22

LAST FOOTBALL GAME/THE INJURY

I t was the next Saturday and the last football game of the season for John and Elizabeth. John's family was in attendance as was his best friend Brian, an African American man, who was a professional football player. Brian spent his entire childhood in Dempsey. He grew up during segregation and lived through a very dark time in history. He learned to say "yes sir" and "no mam" early in his childhood. He learned not to buck a system who seemed to prefer white people. He learned not to stare at white women and to keep his head down when he walked around town. Brian learned to say yes when he wanted to say no and say no when he wanted to say yes. Brian met John in elementary school on the football team. He was a couple of years older than John, but they became buddies early in their childhood. Brian vacationed with John's family and John's mother and father treated Brian as their own. They were 100% colorblind and loved Brian like a second son. Brian was an exceptional football player and taught John a lot about the game. He supported John's aspirations and put in good words for John among all of his football contacts. As much as John loved Brian, Elizabeth hated him. She felt like Brian held John back from his aspirations. Actually, Brian helped John achieve his goals. He was a star football player on a professional football team. Brian promoted John from inside of his football team and Brian was John's biggest fan. Elizabeth had not been exposed to any cultures other than her own. She was shallow and had a difficult time accepting other people who did not look like her. Her family were racists and had taught her to be a racist. She faked her emotions around John, but he knew how she felt about Brian...he was the negro man who John went to school with when he was little. That is what Elizabeth thought. The truth was John loved Brian like a brother. He did not care about the color of his skin. Nor did his parents. He resented Elizabeth for her opinion of Brian. He thought her opinion was cruel and unwarranted. Actually, John resented Elizabeth for most of her opinions. He felt she was an arrogant and mean-spirited person. But, John liked the way she looked and he was shallow enough to overlook her terrible racism. Brian was married to his high school sweetheart and had a little boy named Reggie. Reggie was 7 and seemed to be following in his dad's excellent football play. He was already an all-star football player and was being seriously looked at by college football scouts. At the last football game of the season, Ester, John's sister, was in attendance as was practically the entire population of Dempsey. It was the third quarter and John's team was leading the game. Upon taking the center snap John dove ahead only to be obliterated by the opponent's defensive line. His knee was smashed in the pileup, and John laid on the ground for several minutes before attempting to rise from the pile. When he finally did stand up, his knee failed to support his upper body and he collapsed to the ground. After the moans from the crowd, John was removed from the field by a stretcher. He was conscious but in severe pain from his left knee injury. He was taken to a local hospital where he was met by his family, his friend Brian and Elizabeth, who he had been dating since the picnic in the park. As the doctor entered the room, John paid close attention to what he had to report. Since he had been under the microscope by a few NFL coaches, he grew very worried that this injury may derail his NFL chances. The doctor said to John, "You have a dislocated kneecap and have torn several ligaments in your left knee." John screamed "damn it!" He continued, "Is this a career ending injury doctor?" The doctor explained to John that it could be a career ending injury. It was a Grade III injury – an ACL tear. John lowered his head and sighed holding back tears. Ester grabbed his hand and Elizabeth brushed his bangs from his forehead. John's mother pulled him to her and told him everything would be okay. His dad, in his dad way, punched him in the shoulder and said "no worries son". Everyone in the hospital room knew how important it was for John to play professional football. Nothing else mattered to him. And he never tried to hide his future aspirations. John felt like an NFL contract was his exit out of mediocrity. It would separate himself from the halves and have nots. Although John was comforted by his family, Elizabeth and Brian, no one could make him feel better. Elizabeth was concerned as to how it would affect her future. She had skipped two periods and was pretty certain that she was pregnant. Her seemingly flippant and narcissistic attitude did not sit well with John, Brian or John's family. They talked about Elizabeth, behind her back, and called her a spoiled prima donna. Elizabeth was too clueless to notice that the group was not her supporters. She would think that they were jealous of her. Elizabeth did have a confrontation with Brian at one point. He told her that she was a racist and did not love John. She called him the "n" word and told him to go back to the plantation. That conversation marked the end of any relationship that they could possibly ever have. From that day on, they ignored each other, and any interaction that they had was 100% shallow. After a night in the hospital, John with help from Brian, tried to put weight on his injured knee. His knee buckled under him and he fell to the floor. "Shit! said John. This injury is going to ruin my future...ruin my life! Brian tried to explain to John that he had more than just football talent. John rolled his eyes and said, "Oh yea. I have a college degree in criminal justice. And, a girl-friend who probably only wants to be with me because of football. And, a mother and father who have been bragging to their friends about their NFL son. My life is just GREAT!" John said with aggravation. Brian patted John on the shoulder and told him to hang in there. The next day John was informed that he would have to have arthroscopic surgery that would take a lot of rehab to correct. And, if it was corrected, a brace might have to be worn for a while. Bottom line is that John's injury was not the kind of injury that an NFL recruiter could ignore. The injury was too devastating and had too many long-term repercussions. Bottom line was that John was not the kind of player an NFL recruiter wanted to offer a contract to. John had not totally given up on his football dreams, but he was about 95% sure it would not happen. He was correct about this one thing. The only thing that the injury would leave John with was a lifetime limp that caused sporadic pain and the need for a cane as well as a drug addiction to pain meds. Elizabeth visited John a number of times in the hospital, after surgery, and when he got home. After several pregnancy tests and skipping two periods, she was fairly convinced that she was pregnant. She decided to take John out for dinner and tell him about the news. It was a Friday and John had gone through several weeks of rehabilitation. He thought dinner was a good idea. John and Elizabeth met at a local Italian restaurant that was known for their fettucine. The restaurant was dark and inti-mate…a place where young lovers dine or get engaged. Elizabeth was nervous entering the restaurant and really did not know what to expect. She had decided to tell John that she had taken a pregnancy test that was positive. Elizabeth thought, "This on top of his knee injury could put John over the edge." But, she knew she could not keep the secret any longer She decided that she would have the child. Abortion was not an option for her. She fundamentally disagreed with the procedure as did her entire family. Elizabeth's cousin, Amelia had an abortion when she was 15 years old and her parents spoke very badly about her years after the procedure. As Elizabeth entered the restaurant, she immediately saw John sipping a Pale Ale and staring off. As she leaned over to kiss John hello, her boob fell out of her shirt. John said "hello to you too." They laughed for a moment and then Elizabeth sat down. The mood quickly turned serious when Elizabeth told John she had something to talk about with him. She explained to John that she never intended nor thought that either of them would be in this situation but that she did care about John. "John" Elizabeth said "I am 2 months pregnant." As John wiped the beer that he spit out of his mouth onto his lips he said. "How did that happen?" Elizabeth said "well, we had unprotected sex as I told you a few times." John's shock was apparent to Elizabeth which caused an argument. "I am sorry John, but who said it was my responsibility to have birth control. There are things called condoms." Elizabeth said angrily. John apologized and explained to Elizabeth that it was just really bad timing. "I haven't heard from my agent regarding an NFL offer, and I haven't prepared to take the LSAT test for law school if the football thing doesn't go through. On top of that, I am in a stupor most of the hours in the day from pain meds I'm taking for my knee. On top of that, we are both graduating in December." Elizabeth said that it was not a particularly good time for her either but when is getting knocked up a good time for anyone? He said of course and that they would have to think about their next steps. Elizabeth said "well, my next step is telling my mother and father that their daughter is pregnant by a man they have not even met yet." She continued, "my god John they still think I am a virgin." John said "no they don't". Elizabeth was pissed off even more. Dinner ended abruptly without Elizabeth finishing her meal. John finished his. As he was driving home, John was wracked with fear. The fear of being a young father, the fear of not being able to provide for Elizabeth and their children were his major fears. As John limped up the stairs to his fraternity house room, his roommate yelled, "Hey man. Your agent wants you to call him back." John's heart skipped a beat. As John sat at his desk in his room, he picked up the phone and dialed his agent Dan. "Hey Dan the man" said John. After John asked Dan the news, Dan immediately apologized to John about the long delay in getting back to him. Red flag John thought. This is a precursor to bad news. I have heard this tone before and it was always preceded by bad news. Dan started by explaining that he had spoken to several NFL recruiters initially when John started his football season in college. He explained how high the interest was when John first started playing football. He then pivoted to the knee injury and said the interest in John had faded after his knee injury. Dan told John "Any interest in you as an NFL player has completely eroded. You are a liability to the recruiters I spoke with, and they do not want the risk associated with your injury. I am sorry." John was devastated after the phone call. He was angry. He said nothing to his roommate who he saw as he limped down the stairs to his Jeep. All he wanted to do was get in his vehicle and drive off a cliff. He thought his life was over. He stopped at the Gruber and drank several beers. He then drove the female bartender home and had sex with her. After sex, John hastily left, said nothing to the bartender and slammed the door. He said to himself, I got what I wanted. John went to bed mad, woke up mad and ate breakfast without talking to anyone. John's roommate figured the news from the agent wasn't positive or he would have heard differently. Bad news traveled as fast as good news in the fraternity house, so John figured the boys knew. The next day John woke up and began to think about the pregnancy and the idea of taking the LSAT to be an attorney. He decided since he did not make it into the NFL, he would have to seek other opportunities for his future. Regarding the pregnancy, he thought he could be in a worse situation. Elizabeth was attractive, her family was wealthy, and she would probably accept a marriage proposal since I got her pregnant. He thought if I cannot be wealthy on my own, maybe I could be wealthy through marriage. First step was to sign up for the LSAT class and study for the test. Second, John called Elizabeth and asked her out to dinner. Thirdly, John got a loan for an engagement ring. He thought a one or two carat diamond will not do. But, perhaps a three or four carat would do. He hustled to the Dempsey Diamond Stop. He bought a three carat diamond in a round setting. He called Elizabeth and asked her to dinner. It was the same Italian restaurant where she announced her pregnancy. They both loved Italian food. So, this is where they would go. John bought flowers for Elizabeth and bought a shirt for the night. He thought, "I have to nail this proposal. I'm down to my final option." As Elizabeth entered the restaurant, John stood up to greet her. She asked him what was wrong since he never stood up before. He said nothing. I bought you these. She commented on how beautiful the flowers were and sat down by John. She kissed him on the cheek and grabbed a menu although she knew what she would order. John told her that although he didn't expect this to happen, he was in love with Elizabeth and wanted to marry her. He presented the ring to her and she blushed with excitement and confusion. She said "Wow John. I never expected this!" Thank you." She said yes to the proposal but added a caveat. "John I will marry you, but I need to know that you are not doing this because I am pregnant," John thought, "Of course I am doing this because you are pregnant. What else am I to do?" He said to Elizabeth, "I love you regardless of whether you are pregnant or not." Elizabeth did not believe that John loved her. But, she loved the diamond ring and immediately put it on her finger. She squealed. "I love it!" John was happy. After dinner, John and Elizabeth walked holding hands to their vehicles, kissed goodnight and drove to their sorority and fraternity houses. As Elizabeth walked up the stairs to her room her roommate noticed the ring immediately. "Elizabeth, girl are you engaged?" she asked. Elizabeth said "well, yes I am...as of tonight." The girl held out her hand and Elizabeth gave her a high five. Any details the girl asked? "Not yet said Elizabeth. It's only been a couple of hours." After an early dinner with John, Elizabeth returned to the sorority house and phoned her parents. They seemed happy for Elizabeth, and her mother said they should have lunch the next day to show them the ring. By this time, Elizabeth suspected that John did not get an NFL contract. She thought "perhaps the law school thing will work out for our future." The next day Elizabeth met her mom and dad at a local sandwich shop that Harry owned. "I guess lunch will be free for me, Elizabeth said to herself." After ordering their lunch, the three sat down at a table. The parents commented on Elizabeth's ring and her mother said that John had done really well picking out the engagement ring. Elizabeth agreed. Then Elizabeth told them that John would probably not be getting an NFL contract but would be taking the LSAT test for law school. Although they voiced their collective disappointment at the news about the football contract, they were hopeful that John would get into law school. The three chitchatted for a bit longer and then Harry said he had bowling practice. This is where he met Honey. Honey was the town skank and was married to Warren, the town loser. Harry had tried and failed to recruit anyone in his family, but he enjoyed playing on the bowling league. His league membership was a conversation with some Dempsey residents and his family six months back when Harry was rumored to have been having an affair with someone on his bowling team. That someone was Honey, and Liza threatened to divorce Harry. He denied it even though Liza had found a note written by the woman suspected of having an affair with Harry. They fought...she forgave...they moved on. This was rumored to have happened a number of times with young women, old women, all women. M Harry was sexually insatiable. He did not care necessarily who was available when he needed a sexual fix, he just wanted sex.

Liza felt he was a sex addict, but as long as she wasn't the recipient of his disorder, she did not really care. Elizabeth and John planned their wedding for three months in the future. They wanted to have more time, but Elizabeth would already be showing pregnancy by this time. She would have to make arrangements for her wedding dress to distract from the baby bump. Elizabeth had always wanted a big wedding since she was a child. She dreamed of this special day all her life, but her plans did not include having a child shortly after tying the knot. Elizabeth wanted a large church wedding with eight of her sorority sisters. John balked at the idea and thought it was frivolous except for the bachelor party. He wanted a bachelor party. And, as long as her parents were paying for the wedding, he didn't care how exorbitant it was. The only problem that Elizabeth saw was that John's best friend Brian would be his best man. Normally, a best friend would be chosen to be a best man right? Normally. However, Brian was African American and Elizabeth and her entire family were racists. Brian and John had been best friends since kindergarten. They played summer football together, played sports in school together, shared secrets, went camping and were scouts together and just liked each other! Since Elizabeth knew no one that was African American she didn't get it. John thought, "There is nothing to get. I like him!" The discussion of Brian in Elizabeth and John's wedding created turmoil for the couple. Elizabeth made insensitive comments about the color of Brian's skin, but John blew off her concern and called her a racist. Each time Elizabeth brought up the wedding John would think, "This is going to be the wedding from hell!" Elizabeth laid out her wedding plans and anticipated cost to her parents. They did not flinch with the over a hundred thousand dollars projected cost. Elizabeth was a southern girl and she had been imaging her wedding...minus the pregnancy...for many years. The "have to" items on her list were: invitations, venue cost, flowers, lighting, cakes, open bar, reception dinner, reception band, professional photographer, groom ring, videographer, bride dress, entertainment, guest accommodations, bridesmaids' gifts, and groomsmen's gifts. Elizabeth was good at planning parties. Her work with the Dempsey Junior League was legendary for her attention to detail and planning. According to honeymoon etiquette, the groom and groom's family are responsible for paying for the honeymoon. However, John did not have the money to cover an expensive honeymoon to the Maldives with a bungalow over crystal clear water. That is what Elizabeth wanted. Although John cringed at the thought of his in-laws paying for practically the entire wedding, he loved the thought of getting all of this stuff for free. John matched the number of groomsmen to the number of bridesmaids that Elizabeth would ask to be in the wedding. John didn't know much about any of the brides-maids. He of course knew his groomsmen especially Brian. Everyone who was asked to be an attendant in Elizabeth and John's wedding accepted. They were proud to be asked, although Elizabeth's sorority sisters complained about how "fru fru" the wedding would be and how expensive their bridesmaid's dresses would cost. To Elizabeth's face, her friends acted elated that they were asked to be in the wed-ding. But, behind Elizabeth's back, they called her "a spoiled little rich bitch" and a "prima donna". Before the wedding, Elizabeth had regrets for accepting John's proposal. Of course, she was hot for John, but he was not the kind of man that was on her "marrying list". Elizabeth felt he was really too uncultured to be her husband and the father of her child. John knew how Elizabeth felt and that he was not the most likely husband for her. He did not care. As long as he was affiliated with the Conovers, he would get a lot of free stuff. At least ½ of John's groomsmen had slept with Elizabeth after a drunken night of partying. John knew but did not care. He understood why they would want to sleep with Elizabeth. The wedding planning started the day after Elizabeth received her engagement ring. She began to call venues for the wedding, invite her mother to look at wedding patterns because she wanted her dress made, call seamstress to inquire about timelines and research restaurants for the rehearsal dinner. She wanted to have her rehearsal dinner at a fancy restaurant that served a variety of dinners including beef, fish, and pasta. She would hire a wine sommelier to pick out the wine for her reception. The wedding date was in the month of March after John and Elizabeth's December graduation. This would make her honeymoon in the Maldives great for long days on the beach, snorkeling, and diving. Also, the water would be crystal clear and the weather ideal. One could say Elizabeth was more in love with planning the wedding than marrying John. One would be correct. In the middle of all the wedding planning, life went on. John was studying to take the Law School Admission Test (LSAT) and had moved back in with his parents after graduation, Harry and Eliza were redoing their bedroom and planning a cruise around Christmas. They would take a 14-day cruise and tour Venice and Tuscanny. Although expensive, Liza had wanted to take a cruise since college. She was very interested in the architecture of Venice and Tuscanny. Harry was just interested because it was not Dempsey. Elizabeth was sad that they would be gone for several days around Christmas while John was excited to not have them around for 14 days. While Liza and Harry were on the cruise, Elizabeth and John were to watch the house for any potential problems. Harry had scheduled a pool cleaning and Liza had preordered some window shutters that would be installed when she was on the cruise. She also had a maid that cleaned her house twice a week and a cat that needed to be fed and watered. John and Elizabeth agreed to take care of all of this when Harry and Liza were on their trip. John, of course, bitched about it that instigated an argument between he and Elizabeth. Elizabeth would take up for Harry that would always cause conflict in her marriage with John. "Why do you always feel the need to protect your father? He has repeatedly proven that he is insensitive, selfish and narcissistic," said

John. Elizabeth countered with "He has been extremely generous with us John. Have you forgotten where we were before he helped us out?" John was furious! "How could I possibly have forgotten Elizabeth. You remind me all of the time." railed John. Then he would start his regular speech about his parents and how they respected his privacy and never interfered with the decisions he made. They supported John 100% with his football aspirations and never made him feel embarrassed when he did not get recruited by the NFL. The conversation regarding John's parents would upset Elizabeth. She said "Well John we all know how perfect your parents are and how perfect your life has been with them. But, do you have to bring it up every time I am taking up for my parents?" John told her that this is not what he had intended and then he dropped the subject. A dark silence enveloped the Moss house for hours. Elizabeth felt a tinge of envy and did not know what to make of parents who were not nosy and stayed out of her business. She was privately jealous of John and wished for parents like his. While Elizabeth's parents were planning a cruise to the Greek Isles', John's mother and father were planning a trip to visit their daughter Ester in Colorado where she was attending graduate school. During this time, Elizabeth was pregnant for the first time in her life and living with her parents after graduation. Harry and Liza were disappointed in Elizabeth for "getting knocked up" by John. However, they would privately acknowledge that it happened to them also. Elizabeth was not easy to get along with at this point. She cried all of the time and acted like a complete drama queen. Her morning sickness was moderate and she acted as if it was severe. She was moody and irritable at John and asked him often "why he did this to her". John simply rolled his eyes and ignored her as he did so well. He had already registered to take the LSAT and had little time to study for the test. In order to get into a top law school, he had to score well over 160. The scale was 120-180. He had his study materials and signed up for a test prep class on how to take the LSAT. John appeared over-confident in his ability to score high on the LSAT. He had never been a top student or a strong test taker, but he never lacked confidence in his ability. However, now John's confidence was a little unsteady since he failed to receive an NFL contract. So, in the following month John intended to study hard and put in some long hours to score high on the LSAT. Since John and Elizabeth lived in different locations and John was spending much of his time studying for the LSAT, they spent most of their time together on the weekends. They would have dinner often and frequently and speak on the phone but, Elizabeth was manic about the wedding plans and John was unemotional. Every time John and Elizabeth were together she would talk his ear off about the wedding plans. John became somewhat robotic when he spoke to Elizabeth about the plans. He would agree with every decision she made and said "sounds good" and "okay" to everything Elizabeth said. Although the couple did get on each other's nerves from stress, they often made up by the end of the night. John was feeling a lot of pain from the football knee injury. It made him moody and nervous. The pain meds he was taking for the injury made him jittery, agitated and moody. The pain, according to his doctor, would be with him throughout his life. To help with the pain, John sought to buy pain opioids from dealers on C street in Dempsey. C street was in a sketchy part of town. The street was full of drug addicts, dealers and young college student looking to score some drugs for a night of unsuper-vised partying. C street was known by most of the residents in Dempsey but rarely visited by the majority of the townspeople. After the football injury, John spent a significant amount of time and money on pain meds that he purchased from C street. He turned to the illegal drugs after his doctor had prescribed initial pain meds for John's knee and then refused to refill the drug because he did not want for John to become addicted to the drug. This is when John turned to the drugs he could purchase on C street. The drugs he purchased from C street were extremely strong and addictive and seemed to help John with his pain. However, now he was facing a serious drug addiction. Regardless, John chose addiction over pain. So, as John slowly moved around the house and seemed to take an inordinate amount of naps, Elizabeth was oblivious to John's drug use. She was preoccupied with her current responsibilities of planning a wedding and thinking only of herself and did not have time or interest in checking in with John to make sure he was alright. Time seemed to fly by. John was scheduled to take the LSAT on Tuesday and a month from then was the wedding that Elizabeth had labored over for what seemed like an eternity. Everything was scheduled planned and sewn so it was just a matter of waiting. By this time Elizabeth had felt the baby moving. Although nervous, John felt confident about the LSAT. He had studied, taken practice tests and hired a personal teacher to help him with the test.

CHAPTER 23

JOHN TAKES LSAT

John asked Elizabeth to take him to the test and she agreed. During the car ride to the test Elizabeth went on and on about the morning sickness she was feeling. By that time, John wished he had driven himself. The test was being held at a room in the college where John graduated. He was familiar with the layout of the college and was confident that he knew where the test was being held. But, as he walked into the room where he thought the test was being held, a professor told him the test location had been changed to another room. He received the information and ran out of the room that was across campus. It was now 8:45. The test started at 9:00. He was nervous and rushed now. "Damn it!" John exclaimed frustrated. He arrived at the room at 8:55 and sat down where the test would be administered. He made no eye contact with anyone, took a deep breath and received the test document. The LSAT is a multiple-choice paper and pencil test that law schools use in addition to other criteria to determine your eligibility to be accepted into a law school. It contains a logical reasoning section, an analytical reasoning section, a reading comprehension section and a writing sample. The test would take about ½ day, and John should receive his scores in approximately three weeks via email. "Great" he thought. "I should be expecting my test scores around the time of my marriage to Elizabeth. God help them be good!" John thought. As John settled in to take the LSAT he felt a cold chill run down the back of his neck. He read the first question and thought "This test is not what I thought it would be. It is going to be very hard! I am only on the first question, and I am freaking out!" On many of the multiple choice questions John guessed at the answers. He thought many of the guesses he made were incorrect. His over confidence turned to fear and his fear turned to anger which had been a familiar emotion since the football injury. It was nearing midday and John had finished the LSAT. He met Elizabeth outside and prepared himself for the test inquisition from his future wife. Elizabeth said in her thick Southern accent "well, how'd you do? John replied, "Elizabeth I just took the test. How am I supposed to know?" John said in a sarcastic tone. Elizabeth continued, "Don't have to bite my head off I was just askin!" John corrected himself, "Sorry, it was hard...a very hard test." John finished. "So does that mean you didn't do well?" Elizabeth asked. John continued, "How am I supposed to know Elizabeth!" Elizabeth started crying and said "You don't have to be so mean John! I was just asking!" finished Elizabeth. John interpreted Elizabeth's inquiry as her wanting him to get into law school very much. Under his breath John muttered "so much for unconditional love." Elizabeth asked him what he said. He said "nothing". John explained that he had to go home and help his father with a home project. Elizabeth dropped John off at home and then met her mother at home for a late lunch. Liza had a set of swatches for Elizabeth to evaluate. The swatches represented the potential color of bridesmaid's gowns for the wedding. The dresses were to be made by several seamstresses to meet the tight deadline for the wedding. "How did John's test go", asked Liza. Elizabeth took a deep breath and said "He has been so on edge lately. Bit my head off when I asked him how the test went. I guess okay." "Well, does he think he did well?" asked Liza. "I don't really know" said Elizabeth. "I guess so." Elizabeth's mom was underwhelmed at Elizabeth's response to her question. She was also hopeful that John would get into law school for her family's legacy... and of course reputation in the town. After finishing the LSAT, John took a trip to C street to buy some opioids for his knee. During the transaction, he met one of the dealer's sister who was also there to score some drugs. Her name was Allison. Allison was 26 and had big boobs and a small butt. John liked the way she looked. She took to John too and started a conversation with him. "So" she said. What is your story?" Allison asked John. John explained his injury, his drug preference and his upcoming nuptials that he made sound bleak." "Wow" said Allison. "You are getting hitched in a few weeks?" she asked. "Yes, I am" replied John. "It is kind of a quick deal. She's pregnant." explained John. "Oh, I see" said Allison. You know no one has to get married anymore" she said. "I did not say I had to get married. I just said it was quick because she is starting to show." "Oh I see." said Allison. "Well do you want to have some fun with me?" Allison asked John. She raised her skirt and showed John that she had left her underwear at home. A little taken back John said "sure come over here". After John was finished with Allison, he said goodbye and left with his drugs. As he pulled up to his driveway Elizabeth was there greeting him. "Hayyyy" She cackled. John responded back "How's it going?" Well, I was just wondering what you were doing. You finished your test hours ago." Elizabeth said. "Yes, I took a ride to clear my head." John explained.

CHAPTER 24

THE WEDDING AND HONEYMOON

Elizabeth and John met, and Elizabeth brought over the honeymoon details for John to look at. The information included a brochure from the Vzelement Island resort. M Elizabeth had picked an on the water villa with breathtaking views for only $875 per night. She thought she had selected a good deal since some of the villas were $1,000+ per night. John, unfamiliar with this kind of luxury commented. "This looks good." It was now the week of the wedding. Elizabeth was psycho and John was chill. Everything was booked, sewn, paid for and confirmed. The church was empty and ready for Elizabeth's huge bows and flowers. She had hired a wedding planner who had people place the flowers and bows in the church. She would monitor their every move. Elizabeth went to the church two hours before the wedding. No flowers were there. No bows were there. She flipped her lid, called the wedding planner and cursed her out. Elizabeth didn't know that the decorators generally never decorated the church two hours prior to the ceremony. But, in Elizabeth's world, the flowers would have been there at least several hours prior to the ceremony. The wedding ceremony went fine. Harry escorted Elizabeth down the aisle and winked at one of her bridesmaids who he had slept with in the past. Liza looked pretty in her pink dress with a taupe jacket. And then there was Elizabeth. Elizabeth looked like a princess in her wedding dress. Her bulging stomach did not show, but she still felt the baby kicking all the way down the aisle…reminding her why she was there today. Elizabeth and John took their vows, kissed as man and wife, and exited the church to the car. The reception was extravagant, and it made John feel a little uncomfortable. He felt sorry for his mother and father who blended into the woodwork with their 5+ year old clothes. He seethed at Liza and Harry who were in their hay day as the mother and father of the bride. He never liked Liza. He thought she was shallow. He loathed Harry for his adolescent horniness and abrasive personality. The dinner included the attendees' choice of pork, beef, fish and pasta. Harry chose the pork and bellowed like a pig when he was being served. Liza rolled her eyes and Elizabeth and John looked the other way. After dinner, Harry danced with his daughter and whispered in her ear, "He is getting my girl." A cold chill ran down Elizabeth's back as she nervously replied "yes", and recalled the numerous times Harry had snuck in her bedroom at night when she was a little girl. There was always scary memories that Elizabeth had felt about her father. She failed to remember exactly why but had them nonetheless. After the dance, Liza reminded Elizabeth that it was time to cut the cake. Elizabeth, still reeling from her father's comment, prepped John to join her at the cake table. He did, and the cake was cut. Elizabeth's eyes were red from tearing up at her father's eerie comment. John asked her if she was alright. Elizabeth said "of course." After the cake was served by the attendants who worked the reception, John and Elizabeth changed clothes and read-ied themselves to leave the reception John and Elizabeth would fly to Male the capital of the Maldives in the Republic of Maldive. There was a layover in New York and the entire plane ride was a whopping 20+ hours. John teased Elizabeth, "well, this will give us time to get to know each other." Elizabeth laughed nervously as she thought "boy, is that the truth." In New York with an overnight layover, John and Elizabeth stayed at the Strathmore Hotel a 5-star hotel in the Midtown West area. Both tired from the wedding preparation, the couple overlooked the excessive grandeur of the hotel. 800 thread count cotton sheets with hardwood floors and crystal glasses were overlooked by John and Elizabeth's exhaustion from the extravagant first class plane ride to New York City. After grabbing a quick bite to eat at the four star hotel restaurant, the couple each took a quick bath and headed to bed.

CHAPTER 25

EN ROUTE TO THE MALDIVES

T he next day, Elizabeth and John took a cab to the airport and boarded the flight to Male. Although the flight was basically non-eventful other than a brief turbulence, the couple had sex in the airplane bathroom spastically. Flailing around, as if they had never had sex before, the couple struggled to complete the act. Elizabeth was not in the mood for sex, and John could not get an erection. Over the past months, John seemed to have a harder time in the bedroom. The excessive opioid use was affecting his performance in the bedroom. Elizabeth was clueless and hardly noticed John's difficult time in the bedroom. She was pregnant, and it was all about Elizabeth. She felt unattractive and needed accolades from John much more often. John failed to notice Elizabeth's clues and let her stew in her own self-pity. She commented on how John was eye-balling the flight attendants on the airplane, and he denied it. He was eyeballing the flight attendants and his desire for sex was insatiable. He did not seem to have a problem with sex with anyone other than Elizabeth. Although Elizabeth did not like his flirting, she learned to tolerate John's infidelity like her mother tolerated her father's. Flying first class, John and Elizabeth tried to sleep on the plane between meals. John spent most of his airtime surfing the internet while Elizabeth wrote thank you cards for the gifts she and John received from the wedding. The flight was turbulent at times and Elizabeth complained to John about her motion sickness. John patted her hand and said she would be okay. Her constant complaining drove John mad and he thought "how am I going to get through this marriage with the constant talking and complaining?" So, he ignored Elizabeth and tuned out her voice with headphones the entire flight to the Maldives. Upon arriving at the Male airport, John and Elizabeth exited the plane, asked someone to retrieve their luggage and asked the airport concierge to track down their shuttle to the water plane that would transport them to the hotel that was about 60 miles from the airport. The hotel was on an island so the only way to get to the hotel was to take a seaplane transfer. The hotel was simply stunning. Both John and Elizabeth were overwhelmed when they saw the hotel. The facility was set on a private island on the Indian Ocean. It was a villa on the water with private sea access and a personal valet specifically dedicated to John and Elizabeth. As John and Elizabeth entered the villa they noticed a strong smell of sandalwood and fresh linens. The floors were lined with original teak wood that was velvety and the walls were covered with art that was painted by European artists. The view out of the windows was breathtaking. Schools of dolphins were jumping in the distance in water that was bluer and clearer than either had seen. Elizabeth yawned as she was tired and John was excited as he had never seen a place so beautiful. "What do you want to do now?" Elizabeth said. John replied, "what is there not to do?" He continued "I want to swim, scuba dive, rub oil on my body, rub oil on your body, eat until I am sick and drink until I am sleepy!" From all what John said Elizabeth embraced 5 words "You want to rub oil on my body?" John said "yes" and he changed into his swim trunks. All of the food and drink was catered into the villa. All Elizabeth and John had to do was ask the valet for what they wanted. It was the afternoon of a 7-day retreat in the Maldives. During the trip, John and Elizabeth took naps, went deep sea fishing and took scuba diving trips to view the underwater coral reef. At one point on the trip Elizabeth developed a rash on her upper thigh that oozed and crusted over. John was grossed out. Elizabeth was mortified. The rash resolved itself over a few days, but John could not erase the memory. Elizabeth had a facial and a manicure/pedicure and John had a back and neck massage. On the second day in the Maldives, John and Elizabeth had fever and joint pain. The valet told them it was probably the Chikunguna virus that originates from infected mosquitoes. If they had acquired the Chikunguna virus it resolved on the third day in the Maldives. Elizabeth was most concerned since she was pregnant but the valet told her that the virus was rarely transferred from mother to child. The couple also took a shopping trip into the city that was close to their villa. Elizabeth bought John an expensive pair of sunglasses and a sundress for herself. They ate at a 5-star restaurant and went dancing at a local club. To a bystander one might think that Elizabeth and John were very happy. During the trip, Elizabeth was kind of a drag because she was always tired and felt uncomfortable since she was pregnant. Her low self-esteem weighed heavily on John who she expected to help cure the malaise of low confidence. He quickly realized that there was nothing he could say to help make Elizabeth feel pretty. He thought "she is determined to be miserable on this trip." In the villa next to John and Elizabeth vacationed a couple who lived in Portugal and were celebrating their 15th wedding anniversary. He was a History professor at the University of Porto. She was getting a Master's Degree in fine arts. Since the villas were not close enough to talk without raising your voice, Elizabeth and John would have to practically yell to communicate with the couple. On the afternoon of the third day in the Maldives, John asked the couple if they wanted to have dinner with Elizabeth and he in their bungalow.

The couple agreed to dine with the couple from America. After a brief discussion about American and Portuguese politics, the couples agreed to shelve the political discussion although they were closely aligned politically. The conversation then turned toward discussing the upcoming birth of John and Elizabeth's first child and the Portuguese couple's only child, Joshua. Joshua was the light of the couple's life and they went on for at least an hour about their child. Although Elizabeth and John appreciated the intricate description of the child and every single detail of his life, they both grew bored with the conversation and tried to shorten the dinner with their new Portuguese friends. John had grown accustomed to using Elizabeth's pregnancy as a way to get out of plans the couple had made. He utilized this moment to use his "Elizabeth is very tired." excuse to budge the couple to scoot back to their villa. After the couple left at around 8:00, John and Elizabeth decided to go to bed since they would be taking an early morning champaign cruise. Well, champaign for John. Although Elizabeth had hoped for a more romantic and intimate honeymoon, John was fine with eating, drinking and sleeping during the trip. He was preoccupied with thinking about how he performed on the LSAT test and wondered if his scores were in the mail at home. He was also nursing his injured knee and had brought enough pain pills to last throughout the trip...he thought. As he looked down at the bottle of pain pills he brought on the trip John realized he was running low and started to get nervous as he felt his addiction beginning to take hold. The next morning Elizabeth and John woke up to the sunlight shining in through the blinds in their villa. John opened the door and saw a clear blue sky shining down on crystal clear water. He took a deep breath and felt glad he was there. Elizabeth took a deep breath, kicked a leg out and said "good morning honey." John turned toward Elizabeth and said "good morning sweetheart." Elizabeth was pleasantly surprised to hear the rare romantic platitude from John. "Ready for a boat ride?" she said.

John commented back "You mean a yacht ride?" said John pointing out the opulence of the trip. After the valet served the couple a breakfast of fruit, croissants and salmon, Elizabeth and John dressed and headed down to the yacht for the trip. Elizabeth was cranky due to the pregnancy. John thought "I can get through this with alcohol." John proceeded to drink a ton of champaign on the boat." And, during the cruise, the more he drank, the more belligerent he was to Elizabeth and the boat staff. At one point he made Elizabeth cry. They made up and continued on the cruise. Elizabeth thought "I hate it when John drinks without me. He is such an asshole!" Because she was pregnant, Elizabeth stuck to orange juice and caffeine Free Diet Coke. She asked John if he thought it would hurt the baby if she had one small glass of champaign. He went off on her question. He yelled at her and said "What do you think you idiot. The baby is being developed right now!" Elizabeth was shocked at his response and started crying again. John apologized and let her have a small sip of his champagne. She said "gee, thanks." Overall, the cruise was enjoyable other than John getting drunk and insulting one of the yachting guest on what he was wearing.. After returning to the villa late afternoon, John fell a sleep and Elizabeth read several baby magazines. John woke up in a crappy mood that did not surprise Elizabeth considering all that he had to drink. He was still rather tipsy and had a bad headache. Elizabeth explained the need to get packed up since they were leaving to return home the next day. Elizabeth was happy to be returning to Dempsey. So was John. They both had fun but Elizabeth was feeling very uncomfortable, and John needed more drugs. He had just enough he thought to last him until tomorrow when he returned to Dempsey. He already started thinking about the excuse he would use to tell Elizabeth he had to leave the house. When the couple returned to the villa from the champagne cruise, they started packing up and getting prepared to leave the Maldives. They would be leaving for home tomorrow. They had already said their goodbyes to their next door villa friends at dinner the night before. Their villa valet had packed John and Elizabeth a goodbye box complete with exotic cheeses, nuts, fruits and a fine bottle of cabernet. The next morning, Elizabeth and John took the seaplane to the airport transit company, and boarded the vehicle that would take them to the airport. After a long flight to New York, the couple took a cab to the hotel and passed out without dinner. They were leaving for Dempsey via New Orleans the next morning. Upon awakening in New York, Elizabeth fell ill. She complained of nausea and gas pains and begged John to change the flight arrangements to a later time. "I can't get on a plane feeling like this John" she said. After a couple of hours of John trying to convince Elizabeth to suck it up, he knew there was no way he was going to get Elizabeth on the plane. He changed the flight schedule, and they would leave from New York at 3:00 in the afternoon instead of 11:00 in the morning. Because Elizabeth felt sick, John rushed to a sandwich shop to eat lunch. After ordering a roast beef sandwich, he thought about ordering lunch for Elizabeth, but he was pissed at her for delaying their flight home. He thought, "I will settle in. Elizabeth can wait for me for a change." After lunch, John and Elizabeth rushed to the airport to catch their flight back to Dempsey. John noticed that over one week in the Maldives, Elizabeth became even more of a snob. John could not believe that was possible. It was raining in New York and there was an "old hotdog smell" according to Elizabeth that was making her sick to her stomach. "Where is the beautiful ocean!" she asked John. "Where is the luscious water!" she continued. John said, "about 20 hours on a flight away!" She said, "Oh yea."

CHAPTER 26

ALMOST HOME

A t the airport, the couple rented a car and proceeded to head back to Dempsey, Elizabeth immediately called her parents. Harry put her call on speaker and her mother greeted John and Elizabeth home. John privately scathed and thought. "Why do they have to be a part of every aspect of my life." Elizabeth, making her voice two octaves higher said, 'Hey mom and dad. you have to take a trip to the Maldives. It is stunning!" she continued. Elizabeth's mom told John and her that she still needed to give them Harry and her wedding gift. "We did not see you before you left on your trip so we didn't get a chance to give it to you." She continued, "Will you have dinner with us tomorrow night?" Elizabeth said yes immediately. John rolled his eyes. When they returned from their honeymoon John and Elizabeth would stay at her sorority house until they found a place to live. The sorority approved the arrangements prior to their honeymoon and asked John to stay cordoned in the room to avoid running into indecent women. Elizabeth and John had a room with two beds that Elizabeth demanded they push together. "We are hitched now!" said Elizabeth. Elizabeth was self-conscious about her pregnancy since she had not told any of her sorority sisters. But now, she was too pregnant to hide her large stomach. Although her thin physique had masked the pregnancy at first, you could now clearly tell she was pregnant. Oh well she thought. I am married now. Elizabeth and John woke the next morning at the sorority house. After breakfast, they drove to Elizabeth's parent's house. After greeting John and Elizabeth, Liza and Harry took them into their study and gave them an envelope with John and Elizabeth's name on the front. Elizabeth had speculated that it was a gift certificate to a local furniture store. John had no idea. Elizabeth slowly opened the envelope and saw a document that read "property deed". "What is this?" said Elizabeth. John took the document out of the envelope and said "no way." "They bought us a house, Elizabeth!" exclaimed John. For the first time Elizabeth was speechless. The only catch was the house was right next door to Liza and Harry. John thought, "Naturally." But, he did not care because Liza and Harry were picking up the tab enabling him to not have to buy a house for Elizabeth. "Well, you want to see it? Harry asked. "Of course!" screamed Elizabeth. John nodded. All of the lots in this development were 5 acres with two story houses. There was a community pool, a clubhouse, and a tennis and golf course. The Mid Century Home was inspired by Frank Lloyd Wright. The house had the original radiators and hardwood floors, authentic stain glass window panels, a bonus room on the top floor and a finished basement on the bottom. It had 4 bedrooms, 3 full baths and a three-car garage. The original floor plan of the house was maintained and had been previously owned by an architect who was committed to keeping the home true to its original plan. It was a beautiful house with a baby room that had been already decorated by Liza. By this time, Elizabeth thought she knew the sex of the baby. It was a girl, and her name would be Jessica. Above the door of the bedroom was the letter J. The room was primarily pink and was furnished with the finest linens and a beaded chandelier handmaid from an artisan in Charleston. Jessie's room was next door to John and Elizabeth's bedroom and there was an extra room for a second baby that John and Elizabeth planned to have. John and Elizabeth were blown away by the generosity of Liza and Harry even if they had bought the house to have them close to Elizabeth and John. Elizabeth was due in a couple of weeks and feeling more and more uncomfortable. John was awaiting his LSAT test scores so the atmosphere was rather tense. Of course, they were more than thrilled that they were given a house that was paid for in full, but John felt less relevant than ever. He would think, "What does she need me for?" If Elizabeth was asked that question, she would respond "What <u>do</u> I need him for?" John banked on his LSAT scores to get him into a prestigious law school but did not feel confident that he had scored well enough. After Liza and Harry gave Elizabeth and John their wedding gift, Elizabeth and John started planning immediately for their things to be moved into their new house. Let's see, there was John's treadmill and Elizabeth's sewing table that was rarely used and some nic nacs. Regardless of their use, the items still had to be moved out of the sorority and fraternity houses. Their rooms would be needed to accommodate new members of the sorority and fraternity. It was time for Elizabeth and John to move into the real world of society with bills they would have to pay and problems that they would have to solve. Now, they would be moving into an empty house with no furniture other than what Liza purchased for the new baby. Over the next several days, they had all the heating, air and electrical services put in their name. They would now assume the monthly bills from the new services. This fact was a bitter pill to swallow considering neither had a job and no money. John had brought over sleeping bags from his mother and father's house. They would camp out in their new empty house until they could afford furniture. At least the baby had a bed thanks to Liza. Elizabeth had her bag packed for the new baby and was ready to go at the drop of a hat. She had prepped John for what he needed to do when the baby was born. This was his and her first child, and both of them were freaked out about the prospect of having a baby. But, they understood their roles in the birth. John did not expect the drama that would ensue at the hospital. Elizabeth was dealing with excessive bleeding due to pregnancy induced hypertension. She would be okay, but she was extremely emotional. Her condition was clearly an emergency situation, but she was a drama queen and made it worse than it was. After a few days in the hospital, Elizabeth and John brought home their first child, a boy named Truitt. Truitt was supposed to be a girl named Jessica. At the last minute, John took down the letter J that was above the door to the baby's room. He bought a couple of blue blankets, a pillow, a few stuffed animals and a mobile for above the baby's bed to try and tailor the room more toward a male baby. After John and Elizabeth arrived home with the new baby, they were immediately greeted by their new neighbors Liza and Harry Conovers. Under his breath, John whispered to himself "it has started". He felt like Harry and Liza would take every bit of his and Elizabeth's independence and infringe on their privacy. After a sufficient amount of graveling over the new baby, inspecting the new house, and voicing their opinions about what needed to be purchased to make the house a home, Liza and Harry finally left Elizabeth and John's house. Elizabeth needed to rest and she went to sleep immediately after her family left. John poured a pale ale and checked the mailbox. Included with sales flyers, credit card statements, and other solicitations were his LSAT results. He took a deep breath and with shaking hands opened the envelope. He understood he would have to score at least 160 in order to be eligible to get into a top law school. The number read 122 and John was panicked. He threw the results, drank his beer down and left the house. He was headed to C street where he would buy more pain killers and try to forget about the nightmare he was about to be thrust into. John thought, "what am I going to do now?" After driving home from buying the opiods, John drank another beer, took a pain pill and passed out on the floor.

CHAPTER 27

FAILED EXPECTATIONS

E
lizabeth woke up before John, picked up the baby and went downstairs where John was passed out on the floor. Elizabeth yelled, "John, what is the deal? You did not come to bed last night!" John turned over and muttered to Elizabeth, "I did not score well on the LSAT". Elizabeth said "Oh, I am sorry." John said "Me too!" John felt he had reached the lowest point in his life. Elizabeth felt like she had failed at selecting a husband. They were both right. The day went on with John grueling over poor test scores and Elizabeth visiting her parents to deliver the news about John's low test scores. Liza and Harry were very disappointed with John and his LSAT scores. They had been confident that he would come through and score well on the test, but he did not. Now he was faced with a bleak future. He was angry at the current position in his life. He wondered what he would do now. Elizabeth was reluctant about sharing the news with her parents, but she knew she had to and felt like with her father and mother's money, they could possibly help John. Harry met with John privately and asked him what his plans were for his future. John laughed to himself considering he was being asked about his future from a man whose future was given to him as a birth rite. John explained that he did not plan to be in this situation, but he was regardless. John mentioned to Harry that he

held a degree in criminal justice and could be employed by a local police force. Harry said that he was a top donor at the local police department and that he personally knew everyone on the staff at the Dempsey police department. "I could put in a good word for you there if you would be interested. I spoke with an officer there the other day and he said they have an opening." Harry said. John said of course he was interested especially since all of his plans had dried up. Harry made one call and John was hired as an investigator for the local Dempsey police force. Elizabeth asked John if he was okay with this job. He replied, "Why not? Seems like it is all I can do." said John feeling pathetically sorry for himself. It was Friday. John would start the job on Monday. The police department needed someone new badly. The salary that John would receive wasn't great, but it was okay and it would keep he, Elizabeth and Truitt out of bankruptcy. Plus, he had no mortgage payment. John woke up on Monday morning with faded hopes and a large chip on his shoulder. He told his friend Brian on Sunday that his life had turned out exactly how he feared…with failed expectations and lost goals. He said he loved his son, but he was afraid that Truitt would not want to be like his dad. Brian took the normal stance with John and told him that he should embrace the life he had. He had his health, a wife that loved him and a new child. John said, "yes I do, but that is easy for you to say. You have a contract with a professional football team." Brian acknowledged that John was right and ended the conversation there. John settled into life in his new home. The job at the Dempsey police department included a staff of police and a couple of investigators like John. One investigator was a female who immediately took a liking to John. He liked the way she looked and was excited to be working with a female. Her name was Charlotte but everyone called her Charlie. She was from Flagersville, a small town outside of Dempsey that was just slightly smaller than Dempsey. There were two police officers at John's new job…Derek and Bobby. John liked them immediately. Lucky for John, the guys were not the sharpest tools in the shed so he felt intellectually superior to them. John was complacent but adjusting to his role at the Dempsey Police Department. His role as a criminal investigator was to investigate homicides, bank robberies, kidnapping, organized crimes, extortion and corruption. Considering the size of Dempsey, John's job was boring, but he had a new mortgage free house with a family. Elizabeth was pregnant again with her second child. She felt like a pro now since she had gone through the experience once before. She felt like her life with John was more stable and their lives were ready for a second child. Little did she know that John was emotionally involved with someone at his job named Charlie. John liked the fact that Charlie was independent. Her parents did not live close and she had few obligations since her children were older and not so dependent as his children. Elizabeth loved being pregnant a second time with a girl. She found out the sex of the baby the second time and was happy that her second baby would be a girl. She had dreamed of decorating the nursery in her signature color of pink and decorating the nursery really girly. Elizabeth was surprised that she was pregnant a second time since John had shown very little interest in having sex with her. She wondered if he was turned off from her "first baby body". Regardless, she didn't care. She was thrilled that she was having a baby girl and did not hide her excitement a bit. Jessica Moss (Jessie) was born and was welcomed into the world by excited grandparents and one excited parent…Elizabeth. John remained mired in his self-descent down a dark hole that he would never emerge. Good thing that Elizabeth was oblivious to his depression. She was not a supportive wife but someone who thought of herself first. Now the Moss's had two children. However, they were financially fortunate and could easily take care of two children as well as give them everything they wanted. John and Elizabeth Moss lived on a perfect tree-lined street with basketball nets and children's toys strewn about the perfect yards. It was fall…a season for apple cider, pumpkins and kids wearing costumes for Halloween. A time of optimistic outlooks and dreams of a better year. It was not that way for John and Elizabeth Moss. They were stuck. By this time, they were the parents of two children Truitt who was 5 and Jessica (Jessie) who was 3. Although John had settled into his job as an investigator in Dempsey, he was unhappy in his life. His failed aspirations to become a professional football player followed him since college and, along with a paunch he had developed since he was married, he still felt pain from the knee injury. The knee injury left him with a marked limp when he walked and a serious drug addiction. John believed he had settled for a life with a bitchy wife and two children. He even questioned Elizabeth's judgement in choosing to be his wife. The truth was that Elizabeth resented John for not being the husband she had always dreamed of and for getting her pregnant before marriage. (As if she was 100% fault free.) Her life felt like a prison, and Elizabeth resented John for scoring so low on the LSAT test and for not being an attorney, not making enough money, and for not loving his children as much as she loved her children. She mostly resented John for being ungrateful to her parents who bought them a house, bought his children anything they wanted, and for giving John and Elizabeth all that they had. Although John thought that the children were spoiled by Elizabeth and her parents, he loved the children as much as he could. Jessie was an adorable child with beautiful eyes that twinkled bright blue and Truitt looked like John and had Elizabeth's "signature smile" as she called it. Elizabeth was born into a wealthy family. John was not. His family worked for everything they had and expected John to do the same. John had married into money and instead of becoming the bread winner in his family, he assumed the role of major ass kisser to Elizabeth's parents. Everyday that John lived by his in-laws he felt more indebted to them and less important in his own family. He felt like they thought he was a loser for not being the man that Elizabeth had married or the father that his children deserved. John felt as though he would always owe Elizabeth's parents for his house and allowing their daughter to marry him. The extreme pressure that living by Elizabeth's parents caused John a tremendous amount of stress in their relationship. Their sexual relationship was replaced by Elizabeth bitching about the children and her role as a mother and wife. They butted heads frequently about how to raise the children. John felt like the children were totally spoiled by Elizabeth and her parents. Elizabeth disagreed. She believed the children were lucky to have their grandparents next door. But, what Elizabeth did not know is that the children hated visiting the grandparents. They felt like the grandparents bragged too much and used them to impress their friends. When the children would talk to John about the grandparents and how much they annoyed them, John would just smile. He got it and thought the children were right on. He also thought the children were spoiled. They would spend the summers at private day camp, take trips to Vail in the winter to snow ski and spend the Christmas holiday in New York with the grandparents. John thought "who gets to do that?" I did not. And, everything seemed to be about John. If he did not get what he wanted, he would pout and sulk around the house. He wanted a motorcycle and although Elizabeth was adverse to the idea, she bought him one. He rode the motorcycle a few times and let it rust in the garage. John oversaw the installation of an inground swimming pool even though Elizabeth's parents had a pool next door that he could use whenever he liked. He used the pool infrequently and never helped Harry clean the pool. By this time, John had begun using drugs often for his knee pain. He justified it in his mind by claiming the drugs were the only thing that would ease his pain. But, he never tried to irradicate the drug use. In addition to the knee pain, John found himself in debt to the drug dealers by thousands of dollars. He had lost track of the money he owed for the drugs because he would forget as he used. Elizabeth did not know about John's drug use because she was so self-absorbed. She just thought John was moody. He interpreted her avoidance as apathy. She simply did not care. One time, John crashed his Jeep after falling asleep when he was under the influence of the drugs. Because he worked at the Dempsey Police Department, he was cleared of any crime although the rumor circulated that he was a drug user. Harry questioned John about his drug use after learning the rumor from one of the police officers at the Police Department. He told John that he wasn't sure if the rumors were true but that he better pull it together or get fired. Again, John laughed at the irony of Harry warning John of anything when Harry had consistently used his money to get out of legal crunches. John had grown agitated as time progressed. He had a very hard time tempering his mood swings and was not faithful to Elizabeth causing a major schism in their relationship. By this time, Harry knew that John did not particularly like he or Liza. They would talk about John negatively and wished that Elizabeth had chosen someone else as her husband. The children also started to get on Harry and Liza's nerves. The children would walk into their home without knocking, walk through their garden and pick their flowers, and not close the gates to the fences. As long as the grand-children were quiet, they were golden to the grandparents. But, as soon as the children started acting like children, the grandparents were ready to send them home. This friction with the children cre-ated friction with Elizabeth. She told her parents that they were not allowed to discipline the children. If they had a complaint about Truitt or Jessie they were to address the situation with Elizabeth. Elizabeth said that she would talk to the children. This friction be-tween the children's parents and grandparents created a less than ideal living environment for Elizabeth and John and Liza and Harry. The parallels of Elizabeth and John's life to Liza and Harry's were stunning. They both met at college, both had children out of wedlock and both regretted their decision to spend the rest of their lives together with their mates. There were uncanny parallels that were negative. Both couples were caught up in the image they portrayed to the community and worked diligently to keep up the fake façade that both couples had created. As John settled into his new job and Elizabeth settled into her boredom as a housewife, life in Dempsey went on for John and Elizabeth. He welcomed long hours at the police department and the time he spent there and away from his family. His family and Elizabeth reminded him of what he had never accomplished in his life. Elizabeth spent her time volunteering for the Junior League and other nonprofit organizations in Dempsey. She also continued to play the part of the overworked, underappreciated mother. Although she loved her parents and felt lucky she had allies next door, Elizabeth felt pinned down by motherhood and was not having as much fun as she thought she would. She tried to reach out to her sorority sisters from college, but they were always busy with their own families. Elizabeth was perplexed as to why her sorority sisters were not there for her when she needed them. Elizabeth occasionally asked a few of her sorority sisters to lunch. She heard the same excuse time after time. "Would love to, but the kids have flute practice. Or she heard "the kids have ball practice." She would complain to John and say "they have just forgotten me...me...can you believe it? I have done so much for them!" John would just roll his eyes. He really did not care. The truth was that Elizabeth was heavy company for her former friends to be around. They had their own problems and their own families. And, they had grown up. Elizabeth was still living in the past as a former cheerleader and former President of the sorority...a former friend to many of her sorority sisters. She just didn't get it. Elizabeth was needy and selfish and the girls she hung around in college were not the girls that would be there for her now. John had taken up walking as he had developed a weight issue since college. The massive amounts of beer that he consumed did not help. He could not run due to his college football knee injury so he walked for exercise. He worked up to walking 5 miles a day and had lost a few pounds in the process. Although he was trying to cut back on his caloric intake, Elizabeth had taken a cooking class and was not helping John with his goal of cutting back.

CHAPTER 28

MEETING WARREN AND HONEY

One day as John was walking around Dempsey, he passed an apartment complex with a rundown vehicle being worked on by a man named Warren McGraw. Warren peered through the hood of the car, and John asked the man what he was doing. Normally John would have ignored the man but not today. The man yelled back to John, "trying to get the oil cap off." John yelled "I'll help" and proceeded to help with the oil cap. Successful, the man said "Thank you. My name is Warren McGraw". My wife Honey and I live in an apartment right behind us. John introduced himself and told Warren that he lived about 4 miles from him. He was trying to lose some weight so he started walking. Warren said that he needed to get in shape, but he hated exercise. John told him that he could not do any strenuous exercise because of a knee injury so he took up walking as a low impact way to get some exercise. Warren said "cool, could I keep you company?" John responded to the portly man and said sure" and that they could start tomorrow. Warren agreed to meet John in front of his apartment the next day and they could start. Then Warren asked John if he could meet his wife. Feeling abnormally extroverted on this day, John said "sure". As John entered the apartment, he was greeted by a large woman who dramatically threw her hand out and loudly introduced herself as Honey...as in the "sweet stuff that bees make." John laughed to himself and thought "well, I assumed so." Then Honey asked John if he wanted a beer. John accepted the offer and made a face after drinking the first swallow. He was a beer snob and preferred craft beers. After drinking the beer and an obvious amount of flirting with John from Honey, John exited and returned home. Regardless of the aggressive flirting from Honey and the putrid smell of something dead in Warren's house, John arrived in front of Warren's apartment the next day ready to walk. Warren looked odd in his long shots that bagged off of his waste and the cheap athletic clothes that he wore to walk with John. Warren was proud though. Proud that someone asked him to exercise with him. He did not have many friends so he was happy someone was including him in their activity. John and Warren immediately became friends and hit it off quite well. The main reason that that they liked each other was because John felt superior to Warren. John was not threatened by Warren and thought he could dominate him. Warren and John started walking every day and became more open with each other as time wore on. One day, an attractive female jogger ran by as they walked. John made a comment to Warren about how good she looked. Warren just laughed and said "yea, I haven't gotten much of anything lately if you know what I mean." John responded "Yea, I know what you mean. My wife was a hottie in college. Two kids later she has seen better days." *Elizabeth would be mortified if she heard John say that. She was overly obsessed about the way she looked.* Warren said that he could not remember the last time he was physically attracted to Honey, his wife. He continued, "Don't get me wrong, there was a time where I could not imagine myself with another female. But, she has lost her looks over the years. She is fat and bitchy now!" Warren continued. "She used to pay a lot of attention to me, but now nothing." Warren explained. "She just lies there and doesn't move when I touch her. It is annoying." Warren continued. She is also a bully. When she is mad, she slaps me and calls me names. I would leave her but quite honestly, I am a little afraid of what she would do. John said, "Boy, that is tough man. That doesn't sound like any way to live." Warren said "No, it ain't no way to live. Warren continued, "I never thought I would be the kind of person who would wish her bad luck. But, I do. I wish she wasn't in my life. I would be happier with someone who loved me. Can you believe it? One time I woke up and her hands were around my neck as if she wanted to choke me. She said she was just kidding. But, she scares the shit out of me!" After the walk, John started home and thought about what Warren said. He felt bad for his new friend. What John did not know was that his new friend was a liar. Honey never slapped Warren, and she was not abused by him at all. In reality, Honey was scared of Warren and very unhappily married. Warren was a wife beater and frequently hit Honey. He would always tell her he was sorry, but Honey stopped believing that Warren loved her. It was during this time that she started being more open to extramarital affairs. She started dressing differently and began flirting with complete strangers in her apart-ment complex. Warren accused her of sleeping around and told ev-eryone who would listen that she was unfaithful. Actually it was Warren who was unfaithful. He would frequently sleep with the other bartenders and wait staff at his job. He was an unfaithful hus-band and had a history with people who knew him to be angered quickly and aggressive. Warren was pathologically depressed and had tried to commit suicide unsuccessfully a number of times. One time he ended up in the hospital and was fighting for his life after taking over 20 strong pain pills. All Honey had to say was "Good God. Warren can't even kill himself right." John and Warren had more in common than John knew. Warren's physician told him that the overdose left him with severe brain damage. He frequently used his impairment to illicit sympathy and get what he wanted. John frequently used his knee injury as an excuse to avoid work and play with his children. Warren was a habitual liar. So was John. The men both frequently lied to their wives and maintained sex lives in places other than their homes. Although John graduated from college. Warren did not but told everyone he had. Warren told his family and friends that he had attended college and graduated, was a student with good grades. He told them he had graduated with honors and had endeared himself to most of his college professors. Actually, none of the teachers would know Warren's name or recognize him. One time Warren was shopping with his cousin at a local hardware store and told him the man in the line ahead of them at the check-out was one of his college professors. Warren said "hi...hello" to the man. Sadly, the teacher simply looked at him and said "I'm sorry. Do we know each other?" The professor did not know Warren because he had never attended the man's class. He called the teacher an "asshole" and walked out of the store. Warren was overweight and inactive but told everyone he knew that he was a runner. He did not love his wife but told people he did. The lies went on and on. He was such a habitual liar that Warren could not even remember the truth. He told his mother and father that he worked in a doctor's office. He even went so far as to create a name badge of a fake medical practice to support his lie. When his mother and father would visit, Warren would take them by a doctor's office in Dempsey where he said he worked. He was lying. His parents wondered why they were never invited in to meet his work friends, he would simply lie and say that the office was closed on the days they would visit. His parents thought that Warren was odd. They thought this ever since he was a child. As a child, Warren liked to catch insects and pull their wings off. He would abuse small animals. He was a bad seed his parents would say to each other. He had a short fuse and a long temper. He had a few friends who would put up with his lies and just write them off as "That's just Warren." When he started talking seriously about his bad marriage and bitchy wife someone should have listened seriously. Instead, his friends and John kept their thoughts to themselves. The subject of children came up often when his parents were in town. Warren told them that Honey was infertile due to an accident when she was a child. This was simply another reason why his parents did not like Honey. Not only did they think she was gaudy and rude, but she would never provide them with a grandchild that they had wanted for so long. The real truth was that Warren had portrayed Honey in such an evil way to his parents that over the years they had developed a negative picture of honey. His mother would say "Honey is so evil. She is probably lying to Warren about not being able to have children." Warren's father in his apathetic manner would say "yep, probably so." Warren was a picture perfect clone of his father, a man who was as crazy as a bed bug! Warren's father had also been abusive to his mother for as long as they had been married. He would call it "just keepin the bitch in line". Warren's mother had gotten so use to the abuse that she started believing that she deserved the "punishment" from her husband. Warren's parents never expected their son to be married to Honey very long. But, it had been over 10 years and the couple were still married. Early in their marriage Honey tried to ingratiate herself to Warren's parents. She would buy them gifts for no reason…take up a hobby that she knew his parent's liked and invite them over frequently for visits. But, as time went on, the gifts stopped, the interest in Warren's parents faded and the visits became less frequent. This moment signaled to Warren's parents a declined interest in them and made them angry. As time progressed, more attention was given to Warren's bad behavior. The lies started revealing themselves to Warren's family and they became keenly aware of his unhappiness. But, nothing was done. He continued to abuse Honey, while accusing her of being the abuser. Warren's lies began when he was in elementary school. He told his friends that his parents were wealthy and lived on a sailboat in Tampa Bay, Florida. Warren's parents were actually blue-collar workers who had not been raised very well. They were taught that it was okay to lie and cheat as long as you get what you want. Consequently the choices they made were not the most proper and not always legal. When Warren was growing up his parents relied on welfare checks to pay for things. Lying was a way of life for Warren. In order to impress his classmates, he would tell them outrageous lies about his life...the luxurious gifts he would receive from his parents, the trips that his parents would take him, the foreign countries he visited...all lies. As Warren and John continued to walk, John confided in Warren that his life had not turned out the way he thought it would. It was filled with disappointment and false hope that had almost driven him to the edge. Warren reciprocated and told John that he was miserable with Honey and that she was so cruel that he could not see living his life with her. Warren was planting a seed in that he was hoping that John would offer his help in hiring someone to do Honey in. Warren had reached the end with Honey. There would be no reconciliation. Warren's new goal was to dump Honey, find a new wife and quit his job. What Warren failed to admit was that Honey was smarter than his was and knew that Warren had a game plan that did not include her. As John walked with Warren, he listened to his new friend who was obviously unhappy in his marriage. John was bitter and angry enough to open his mind to the thoughts of doing Honey in. He never recommended murder to Warren. But, John thought that it might be the only way to rid Warren of Honey. Because John seemed so opposed to mentioning the subject of murder to Warren, Warren thought what he was going to have to be more aggressive. So, he thought what the hell. I'll just mention the subject to John. Warren nervously said to John "I would think that because you are in the field of law enforcement you probably know some questionable people who are not above getting rid of someone for money." John replied, "Wow Warren. I am not sure that I couldn't get in trouble for just talking about murder for hire." Warren continued. "Well it is certainly something that would not be my first choice, but I am so unhappy." John continued, "Why don't you just divorce her Warren?" Warren explained, "I am one of those screwed up people who can't imagine her with anyone else. Plus, she scares me and I'm not sure that she wouldn't kill me first." John asked Warren if Honey had given him a reason to be scared of her. Warren said "Well, yea. I have woken up several nights with Honey staring over me like she wanted to hurt me." John asked "Has she ever said she wanted to hurt you Warren." Warren explained, "No, but it just seems like she wants me gone." John thought, "well, I really need more than that, but it really doesn't matter if he wants her gone.' John told Warren that he did know some questionable people who are not above murder for hire. He told Warren that it would cost him and Warren immediately began thinking about where he could get the money. He asked John "how much would it cost?" John said that he didn't really know how much it would cost but most likely the lowest end would be $5,000. John said "I know some pretty scummy men who would kill anything for $5,000. But, I cannot be anywhere close to the incident...neither could you for that matter." After getting down to the specifics, John told Warren that he would put feelers out and find out if there was anyone who would be willing to kill Honey for money. Warren grimaced at the $5,000 amount and asked John "do they take credit cards?" John said "no man, hit men don't take credit cards." It has to be cash. Warren did not know where he would get the $5,000 but finally decided that he would steal the money from the bar where he worked. John thought that Warren was a loser and desperate for friendship. He also said that Warren's wife was a piece of work and trashy. John did not mention to anyone Warren's inquiry into a hit man. He knew Elizabeth would not react well to that question. But,

Elizabeth liked to hear dirt on people so she was interested in Honey and Warren. When she got bored with the topic, Elizabeth would change the subject to herself of course. She told John that she worked all day on her Junior League project and was so tired that she put a frozen pizza in the oven for dinner. John rolled his eyes and thought "You don't have a job Princess. Why are you so tired?" He then told Elizabeth that he would find something else to eat since he was watching his weight. Elizabeth said "okay, whatever." She was never particularly interested when the conversation did not include her. Elizabeth never had to worry about her weight. She was naturally thin, beautifully fit and extremely pretty. Frustrated, Elizabeth yelled for Truit to come eat. Elizabeth was pregnant with her second child and moody, emotional, and bitchy like she was with her first child. Truitt yelled "I don't want pizza!". Elizabeth broke out in tears and John ignored her. "Truit, you will eat what I make." yelled Elizabeth. Truit said "No I won't." Elizabeth walked away without a word. Harry and Liza visited Elizabeth and John and walked in without waiting for a greeting. The two families were estranged and did not trust each other. Walking into his house without being greeted was annoying for John. Elizabeth faked excitement and welcomed her parents in. This would cause an argument between John and Elizabeth later. "How are you guys?" said Liza. She continued "I was at the Junior League today and we must have just missed each other. They told me you had just left." "Yea." said Elizabeth. "I was working on the Christmas Ornament Program for the tree." "Really" cackled Liza. "Are you doing it by yourself?" asked Liza. "Yes" said Elizabeth. "I am so bored around here. The JL (Junior League) gives me something to do" said Elizabeth. John overheard the conversation and said below his breath "god forbid you get a real job." He was frustrated that Elizabeth who did not have a job but had a housekeeper and a nanny. John asked Harry what he was up to. Harry explained that he was planning a cruise for he and Liza to the Greek

Isles. It was a 13-day cruise through Barcelona to Venice and they would spend Christmas there this year. "Good" thought John. He was relieved to know that he would not have to deal with Elizabeth's parents over the holidays. "The nagging, the complaining, the snooping. I will not miss Harry's constant berating and grilling me about what I need to do around the house." John thought. John felt like he was indebted to Harry since he was given the house. And, there was a lot of unspoken anger between the two of the men. Elizabeth and Liza felt like they lived in the middle of the two men's animosity towards one another. Because Harry bought John a house, he thought that he had a right to nag John about everything that needed to be done. John would then bitch to Elizabeth about her father's aggressive demeanor. Elizabeth would say "That's daddy." John wanted to vomit. Harry asked John if he had contacted the overhead garage door company to make sure that they serviced the doors this year. John would say "That is on my to-do list." Harry would ask John if he had replaced the basement windows that were cracked. John would say "That is on my to-do list." Elizabeth would say "boy that is a long to-do list John. You sure you didn't bite off more than you could chew?" John rolled his eyes at Elizabeth's comment. She would simply say "That's daddy and where is this to-do list that you are talking about?" John would roll his eyes at Elizabeth and tell her that the to-do list was her father's. John grew tired of Harry's demanding attitude. Over time, John started hating Harry for his authoritarian attitude. When he saw Harry walking up the driveway, he would close the window blinds and not answer the door. When they were in bed that night John brought up Elizabeth's parents. John said, "Liz, your parents need to call us when they want to come over. It is an invasion of privacy to not let us know when they are going to drop in. And, they need to lay off on the bossiness. I did not marry your parents, I married you." John told Elizabeth that they order him around like he is a child. Elizabeth told John that he needed to stop acting like a child. This caused a fight. John said "Elizabeth, I resent that!" He continued, "I am not used to hands-on parents like your parents. And the bossiness, my god!" Elizabeth turned on the water works and said, "John, my parents have been so generous. They bought us a house and most everything that we have. Aren't you being a little ungracious?" John reassured Elizabeth that he was aware of all that her parents had done for them and that he was not ungracious. He thought to himself "How could I forget everything that they have done for us? They remind us all of the time." John and Elizabeth fell asleep will ill feelings toward each other. It was the holiday season, and Harry and Liza were finalizing their cruise plans to Venice and Barcelona. They would fly to Fort Lauderdale from New Orleans on Monday and return to Dempsey 14 days later. On the cruise, they would stay in a premium stateroom complete with a private concierge and masseuse as well as their own chef. Harry was into an all frills vacation regardless of price. Liza liked dining with other guests and meeting new people. Harry did not care about meeting anyone. Upon arriving in Florida, they proceeded to their departure destination and checked into their upscale accommodations. On the second night of the cruise and after consuming a couple of glasses of champagne, Liza told Harry that she had received a call from someone named Honey who claimed she was raped by Harry. Liza was determined to give him the opportunity to explain himself. Harry gasped for air and denied the allegation. He was completely blindsided by Liza's accusation and was speechless – a rarity for Harry. Liza became furious with Harry and told him that his response was completely predictable and lame. After her first accusation and his response, Liza told Harry that she was going to leave him when they returned to Dempsey and tell all of their friends that Harry had raped someone he was having an affair with. Harry explained to Liza that Honey was a gold digger who had bribed him into giving her money to keep her lie a secret. Liza did not buy it. She told Harry that he had been screwing around on her for years and she had overlooked the infidelity. "Harry, I have put up with your shit for almost 50 years, and I am sick of it! I am going to tell our friends and as many people in the town who will listen that you are not who you claim to be. You are a cheat and a fraud. And, I hope that Elizabeth never talks to you again and you are ostracized by the people in Dempsey. Harry was out of breath and panicked. He begged Liza to forgive him and to not tell anyone what he had done. He said he was screwed up and had been since he was a child. He said that he had mental problems and needed help. Liza told him to get over it and that he was not the only person in the world who was experiencing mental problems. She reminded him of his child who had experienced a tremendous amount of trauma. "Elizabeth has experienced more trauma that anyone in this family. Liza continued "Harry, you are too selfish and evil to think of someone else's trauma that you caused!" Liza refused to be coddled by Harry who would normally baby her during an argument. Although Liza was very angry, she said she would complete the cruise as long as they stayed separate and Harry would pay for an extra cabin where Liza would stay. She told Harry that plans had been made for him to move out of their house in Dempsey. His bags were packed and in the extra bedroom. Liza told him that she had been making preparations for weeks and that there would be no reconciliation. She did not love him anymore and was sickened to think of spending one second more with him. Harry told Liza to not be rash. Liza laughed and said "You have to be kidding me. I have been rational throughout our marriage, and I'm over it! All of the girls...the infidelity...the extramarital sex! How dare you! You never once pleased me! I am a laughing stock of Dempsey for staying with you as long as I have." Harry was blown away by Liza and how angry she was. He had never seen her so mad. She never cursed before unless she was angry. He knew she was correct about all of it. After several hours of yelling and accusations, it was bedtime. Liza insisted that Harry sleep on the cabin couch. He said "what about my back?" Liza screamed, "I don't give a crap about your back!" The next morning the concierge brought Harry and Liza breakfast and was welcomed by two estranged people who looked like the night had not been restful for them. The conversation that morning began with Harry graveling over Liza and telling her how much he loved her. He acknowledged that he had a problem with fidelity and thought he was a sex addict. Liza wasn't buying it. The only thing that Liza said to Harry was that she was 100% sure that she did not love Harry and had never loved Harry and that she expected to get a significant portion of their income in a divorce settlement. Liza continued. "You were a terrible father Harry. You never participated in Elizabeth's life, and you ignored her terribly." Liza said. Unfortunately, I cannot make her disgusting past with you go away. But, I will spend the rest of my life apologizing to her for the terrible father you have been." Harry was taken back. He was nauseated and grabbed his chest as if he was having a heart attack. Liza also told Harry that since he had a habit of drooling on himself to keep his mouth shut on his way down. She continued. "Oh yea, and watch the furniture. We don't want a charge for damaged furniture." Liza said she needed air and went outside. Harry sat down on the cabin bed. He thought "I hate that bitch. She has done nothing but ruined my good times and prevented me from being happy. No one could blame me if she slipped and fell off of the boat. Accidents happen." No one knew of the fights between Harry and Liza except for Ted, the Northeastern Retired Doctor who Liza had entrusted in. Liza told Ted how unhappy she was and how terrible Harry had been to her. She told Ted about the affairs Harry had throughout their marriage and how selfish he had been since they were married. She also told him why she and Harry Jr. were married and how he had raped her on their first date. Ted being the consummate gentleman and generally a good person was appalled. He was also angry as he liked Liza and thought she was a good person. Lisa had not shared her feelings about Harry Jr. with anyone in Dempsey. But, she really liked Ted, who lost his wife to cancer two years back. Ted had two boys…one a physician and the other an attorney. Liza felt intellectually compatible with Ted and felt that she could trust him. This was his first cruise since his wife's death and the only one he had ever taken without her. Liza was the only female he had been remotely interested in since his wife's death. Conversely, Ted was the only man who Liza found herself attracted to ever. Any attraction to Harry was at best lukewarm. Ted was authentic and real to Liza. He listened to her frustrations and made her feel like her opinions mattered. Ted was a sounding board for Liza's frustrations. But, the attraction went much deeper. She was smitten with Ted who was everything she had ever wanted. He was not judgmental and let Liza talk without interrupting her. This was a welcome surprise for Liza as she could barely get a word in if Harry was talking. During the cruise, Ted gave Liza his address and asked her to write him. He also added his phone number in case she was ever on the East Coast. Liza felt like a silly school girl with Ted and started imaging how she could see him again. After a shower, Harry went outside to look for Liza. He thought to himself. "A boat accident involving Liza would not be my first line of defense, but I cannot go through a town scandal. I just can't." As Harry Jr. approached Liza and Ted, he was surprised at the jealoushe felt when he looked at the two. Then he felt mad at Liza for accusing him of sleeping around when she was talking to another man. Regardless, Harry walked up to Liza and Ted and asked Ted if he would give he and his WIFE a minute. Liza was furious that Harry interrupted she and Ted. She hoped that he would not leave after Harry's question. She apologized to Ted and said she would talk with him later. As Ted walked away from the couple, Harry immediately started accusing Liza of flirting with another man. Liza was appalled and told Harry to shut up. She told Harry that Ted was more of a man than he was and decent unlike Harry. Harry said "What does that mean?" Liza simply said "oh I suppose the word "decent" is foreign to you." Harry Jr. said as he rubbed his head, "what is that suppose to mean?" Liza said "nothing and told Harry that he had a tremendous amount of audacity to accuse her of flirting with another man when he has been screwing other women for years. Harry turned red and told her "Yea, but you are being mean!" Liza laughed at his immature comment but wasn't surprised. Liza said "Oh, am I being mean Harry? Have I hurt your fragile feelings? Well, now you know how it feels to be treated like shit!" Harry Jr. wondered if she had disclosed her anger to Ted. "He could be a problem." Harry thought. Liza had told Ted that Harry Jr. was unfaithful throughout their marriage and had been accused by someone he slept with of rape. Ted was appalled by Harry's indiscretions. Ted thought that Harry was a horrible man and could not understand how he could treat someone like Liza the way he did. Liza had also told Ted that Harry Jr. was a horrible father and neglected their child. Ted felt very sorry for Liza and hugged her. She trembled with excitement when Ted put his arms around her. She could not remember when she felt so protected…so turned on. Harry Jr. walked up to Liza and Ted looking disheveled and emotionally unhinged. Tripping on his unlaced shoestrings Harry said, "Liza, can we talk down the way a bit?" Liza responded back and said "Ted, would you excuse us?" Ted reciprocated with a "yes, of course" and exited to the right. Harry grabbed Liza's arm, and she pulled away instantly at his touch. "Don't touch me Harry!" she said loudly. Harry pulled away and gave Liza a frustrated and confused look. He steered Liza to an isolated area of the boat and began begging her to reconsider her accusations about him. Liza said to Harry, "You know, the first decade of our marriage was bearable. "Brutal yes, but bearable. I never got used to your friends slapping my ass when they were visiting. But, the marriage was tolerable as long as I kept my mouth shut and did exactly what you told me to do. And then, the rumors of infidelity started flooding in. I mean really Harry. I don't know how you found the time to be so unfaithful with so many women. Everywhere I went I was approached by someone esaying they either slept with you or knew someone who had slept with you. You are such a sleeze bag Harry! I feel betrayed and sickened by your behavior. And, by the way, the people who you think are your friends, are not. I've spoken to many of your "friends" who call you an unfaithful man who is mean and cruel. Really, they laugh at you behind your back. And, if I have it my way, no one in Dempsey will ever trust you again…not that they ever did. I am sick of your sleazy behavior and tired of it all. I intend to ruin you in our community. I will tell everyone who will listen that you have screwed around on me for years and have tried to manipulate Elizabeth all her life. You have no sense of decency, commitment or morality! The final straw was when I received a phone call from someone you screwed. She told me you raped her, and I believe it. Remember, you have a history of rape as I can personally attest. She did not leave her name, but I bet I can guess who it was. That was the moment that I had enough. I grew a backbone at that moment, and I want a divorce as soon as possible." Harry was speechless, and angry. He told Liza that she was unappreciative of his generosity. He allowed her "senile mother" to live with them before she died. Liza responded "you never liked my mother because she had your number! She knew that you have been unfaithful to me for our entire marriage, and she hated you for it. And, speaking of my mother, I am pretty certain that you pushed her down the stairs that caused her death! I am going to see about opening a criminal case against you! And, I have a witness that will swear you were right there when she fell. The person who will testify against you is someone you have treated like crap all of her life." commented Liza. "Is it Elizabeth? Harry asked. She is a coddled brat and has gotten everything for free all of her life." Harry Jr. said. Liza commented, "that coddled brat knew who you were and loved you in spite of your horrendous behavior. She loved you in spite of your screwing around with her friends, my friends and all of the other ladies from the community." Harry Jr. raised his voice to Liza as his face turned several shades of red. Liza could tell the anger was from embarrasement. Harry pleaded with Liza. "Liza do you realize what this could do to me...our businesses...our livelihood?" Liza responded "I don't care about any of that. The money, the businesses, the shallow friendships in the town. All of it can go away! I want OUT!" Realizing that Liza was serious and that her threats were real, Harry bent down and acted as if he was tying his shoelace. He grabbed Liza's thin calves and pushed her overboard the cruise ship. As she hit the water, she was flailing her arms and screaming. Harry sent her off with a "good riddance" comment. Her screams were muted by the Mariachi band playing on the ship. The water below turned red as the impact of the fall had opened an abrasion on her leg that she had gotten from gardening in Dempsey. The blood was misleading and at this point Harry Jr. was convinced Liza had been fatally injured and would eventually drown. Fortunately for Liza, the abrasion was superficial. Unfortunately for Harry, the abrasion on her leg was superficial. After seeing the water turn red from Liza's fall, Harry thought incorrectly that Liza was dead. He thought "No way she could have lived through that fall." But, Liza was not dead... she was pissed! After catching her breath, she swam furiously toward nothingness. Liza knew one thing. She was not going to die that day. She knew the odds were not good in her favor, but regardless she would fight for life. For the first time in her life she wanted to live more than anything. She wanted to live to see justice for herself... for Elizabeth. Liza wanted to see her grandchildren grow up and she wanted to see Ted again. Luck was in her favor on that day. Liza saw something in the distance as she swam furiously. What it was she could not tell...could not see. As she swam toward the item in the water, she noticed she was running out of energy. Her thin arms burned liked they were on fire. Her legs seared with cramps. As she swam closer to the item, although exhausted, she felt hope for the first time since her fall a few hours ago. She saw a float belt in the water. She could not believe her luck. It was an item for water aerobics or pool exercises. Why it was in the water she would never know. But, she was lucky it was there. It was a flotation device that would allow her to take a break from swimming. As she put the device around her waist, she realized that the belt was too big for her slim waist. But, she doubled it up and it did what it was supposed to do. It kept her afloat. Liza continued to float in the water for a few more hours. Although she was tired and at times hopeless, Liza never gave up hope that she would live through this horror. Although Liza was very emotional and sad, she never lost hope. She found retribution in her survival. And then, Liza heard the putter of some kind of ship in the water. At first, the noises were distant, but the boat came closer and she began screaming to attract attention to herself. It was an Indian navy vessel searching for people from a sunken barge. As the vessel approached Liza, the men on the boat threw Liza a lifeline, and she was saved. She was very thankful to the men who saved her. The captain of the vessel asked Liza if they could call someone for her. Liza instantly remembered the phone number that Ted gave her. Liza retrieved the waterproof phone case around her waist and found Ted's phone number. She thought she would not make contact with him since he left the cruise for home on the afternoon of the boat accident but it was his cell and she left a message. Liza did not want to call her home and get Elizabeth and John upset. Plus, she did not want to attract any attention to Harry who was still alive. In the meantime, Ted had retrieved Liza's message. He tried to contact the boat that she had described and finally made contact. On the phone, Liza said "Ted, are you there? I need help. Harry pushed me overboard the ship and I was picked up by a Indian Naval vessel. Ted quickly responded "I know what happened Liza, and I am coming for you as soon as I can get there." Liza felt a sweet sense of safety near Bogatell Beach situated between the Nova Icaria and MarBella beaches in Barcelona. Because her hands were shaking so badly, she dropped the phone, but quickly picked it up and resumed her conversation with Ted. Ted asked to speak to the captain of the vessel. While on the phone Ted asked where the boat was going and where he could pick up Liza. The captain gave Ted co-ordinates to a barge drop off location and Ted took the directions. The location was a few hours away and Ted immediately booked flight and car rental reservations for his trip. He also made flight arrangements for two to New Orleans where he and Liza would pickup a rental car and drive to Dempsey. Ted was very angry at what had happened to Liza and experienced rage like never before. He told Liza to just hang in there and know you are safe now. As the boat that Liza was on continued to head to the barge where they would stop, she tried to stay calm, although it was difficult. Although wanting to remember all of the terrible times in the marriage to Harry, she recanted Elizabeth's birth, holidays, and gymnastics events. She thought about the day she saw Elizabeth take her first step and the first time she said "da, da" to Harry Jr. After this, she pulled herself together and said "those things meant nothing when I was with Harry Jr." Hours later the boat that Liza was on docked at the barge where Ted said he would meet her. As the boat stopped, the captain and crew had to restrain Liza who was super excited to see Ted. As she tripped on the steps leading up to Ted, he grabbed her and led her up to him. He embraced Liza and she started crying hysterically. She thanked him and told him "I know I don't know you well, but I love you." Ted reciprocated and said "I love you too!" They left the boat hand in hand and left for the airport where they would take off in an 1 hour and ½. They would fly to New Orleans and drive to Dempsey. As they entered the plane, Ted used his medical skills to check Liza's vitals.

He checked her blood pressure, her temp and heartbeat. She was fine…a little scared…but fine. After landing, Ted retrieved the rental car he had reserved for the trip to Dempsey. But, they were not going to Dempsey. Not immediately anyway. They were staying at an upscale hotel along the way. The hotel was about 30 minutes away from Dempsey and Liza had no idea what Ted's plans were. As they entered the parking lot for the hotel, Ted looked at Liza and told her that "you will never have to worry about being treated badly by anyone again." Liza simply said "Thank you." Ted then gave Liza a passionate kiss that she could not remember ever having. As they entered the lobby of the hotel, Ted asked Liza how she wanted to handle the room situation. She exclaimed "I want you to get one room for both of us!" Ted was happy. He had a plan that he had devised immediately after finding out that Harry Jr. threw Liza over the cruise ship, and he was thinking of that plan now. Ted made sure he knew the address of Liza's house. He then asked her about the layout of the house in a way that she would not suspect any wrong doing on Ted's part. He said he was interested because Liza told him it was a Frank Lloyd Wright and he too was interested in "organic architecture". After entering the hotel room, Liza took a long hot bath and Ted was thinking about his next Steps. After her bath, Liza met Ted in the room and got dressed in front of him. Any shyness that she felt by being naked in front of Ted melted off. She wanted to be 100% transparent with Ted, the man she believed she believed she was falling in love with. Ted was drinking a cup of coffee and finally addressed Liza. He said, "Liza, I have a relative that lives relatively close to here. I haven't seen the man in ages. I thought I would give you some time to yourself and visit him. Do you mind? Liza actually had to process the question. She was not used to anyone asking her if she minded anything. She said, "Of course not Ted. I am so tired I will probably take a long nap. Ted replied "you sleep and rest Liza. I am sure you need it." As Ted readied himself to leave, he grabbed his keys, his coffee, and the notes he had taken when Liza was describing the layout of her house. He kissed Liza goodbye and grabbed a map on the way out of the hotel. As Ted entered the car to leave, he felt in his pocket for a syringe and a bottle of medication he had gotten before he picked up Liza from the boat where she was retrieved. The meds he had in his medical bag allowed you to feel pain but not be able to talk. "Got it." Ted said to himself. Ted drove faster than he probably should have, but he was in a hurry. He passed the exit where he told Liza he was seeing his relative and saw the exit to Dempsey about 40 minutes from where he began his trip. It was close to sunset, and Ted wondered what Liza was doing. As Ted took the Dempsey exit, he became a little nervous but was determined to complete his task. Prior to leaving the hotel, he had asked Liza the layout of the subdivision where she lived. She had provided Ted with a copius amount of detail related to the neighborhood. Ted took the exit and roughly followed Liza's description of where her house was. 812 Furnish Blvd. Ted recalled. As Ted parked away from the house, he noticed a light on in the house where Liza lived. He parked on the street in the clubhouse section of the neighborhood. As he was walking up to the house, he noticed a man exiting the house with a small dog. It was Harry Jr. walking his dog. Ted quickly turned away to avoid the man. Ted wondered how long he would have to wait for Harry to return. In the meantime, John had left his home and proceeded to walk toward Harry's house. John knew Harry's schedule of walking his dog prior to going to bed so he waited for Harry to come home. So did Ted. Ted wondered who the man was that was now at Harry Conovers's door. Ted watched the man and wished he would have asked Liza if there was anyone visiting them. Harry Jr. was settling into his home when he remembered he had to walk the dog. Hen claimed he didn't like the dog, but he walked him every night, took him to the vet regularly, and fed the animal everyday. He did not however clean-up after the dogs "remains of the day". Harry

Jr. claimed that the exorbitant taxes he had to pay should cover cleaning up after the dog. Harry Jr. grabbed the lease, leased the dog and headed outside to walk the animal. As Harry walked his dog, he constantly felt like someone was watching him. He became ultra paranoid and sped up his walk. Finally, Harry Jr. and his dog made it to the front door of his house back from their walk. Relieved that he was inside of his house, Harry Jr. fell on the couch and breathed a sigh of relief. He did not know why he was scared, he was just scared. In the meantime, John was returning some tools to Harry Jr. so he knocked on the door. Harry Jr. hid his head in the couch cushions until the knocking stopped and he knew whoever was at the door was gone. He was happy when the knocking stopped. He then took a deep breath and said "finally." John said "whatever" and walked home. He threw Harry Jr.'s tools on his porch. That was the way he returned Harry Jr.'s things. The two men had grown apart over the years and Harry Jr. thought John was irresponsible and cheat to his daughter. Ironically, Harry Jr. was a cheat to his daughter's mother. John and Harry Jr. had missed each other this night. But, there was another person outside waiting for the house to clear-out. Ted was near the road in front of Harry Jr.'s house. He had been in the business of saving lives for over 30 years. But, today he was an angry man....a man who wanted revenge for someone he thought did not deserve to die. Ted noticed the front door opening and hid for a minute until he realized he needed the door to open to get in the house. Ted quickly ran to the front porch as Harry Jr. was exiting the front door to see if anyone was there. He immediately noticed the tools that had been strewn about on the front porch. Harry Jr. said "That son-of-a bitch John throwing my tools around. Damn him." John wasn't there so it was a wasted emotionally outburst. But as the door slowly closed, Ted grabbed the spine of the door and held it open so he could enter later. As Harry Jr. proceeded back into the house, Ted held the door ajar slightly until Harry Jr. walked into the house by the bar. Ted had already prepared his neuromuscular blocking agent in his syringe before he arrived at Harry Jr.'s house. Ted wanted for Harry Jr. to be incapacitated yet aware of the harm he would do to him. As Ted slowly entered the house, he noticed Harry Jr. was busy pouring himself a drink at the bar. Ted walked quickly to Harry Jr. and inserted the syringe into his back. Harry Jr. yelled "hey, hey what is going on". Then he passed out. When Harry Jr. woke up he was confused and couldn't feel or move his lower body. He could understand what Ted was saying. But he was unable to communicate with him. Ted asked Harry Jr. if he recognized him. He blinked his eyes in a way that Ted recognized was a yes. Ted continued, "I am the man who is going to pay you back for hurting your wife on the cruise ship. You will never hurt her again. And, by the way, your marriage it over!" As Harry Jr. was writhing on the ground, Ted took his surgical knife out and cut off Harry Jr.'s finger with the ring still on. Ted wanted to give it to Liza although he had not decided on this yet. Harry Jr. was hysterical but quiet for once. He did not bleed out...YET.

Ted continue his informal surgical procedure on Harry Jr. He removed all of Harry Jr.'s sexual reproductive organs including his penis, prostate, and testicles testicles. Harry Jr. then bled out and Ted said "It's over Liza" Ted made Harry Jr. suffer in a manner that he was never accustomed to. He wanted Harry Jr. to suffer like he had never suffered before. He hoped that the pain he suffered was as severe or more than Liza had suffered throughout her life with Harry Jr. After Ted was completed with his "task in Dempsey, he made sure nothing could be traced back to him. He cleaned the tools he used, wiped away any evidence of fingerprints and disposed of any body parts that were useless to his task. He then found a box in Harry's closet that included a number of whatnots from his affairs. He then put Harry Jr.'s finger with the wedding ring in the box and put it in a gift bag that he found in the closet. Then, Ted left. The End

SENSE OF PLACE

Bettye M. White (a passage from my mother's writing) I learned to love Louisiana on the sleepy streets of my hometown. Where I spent my childhood dressed in someone else's hand-me-downs. Having my hair done in our one and only beauty shop where the girls got the Prom queen special and the guys the military flat top. Local gossip was rich and homespun at the shop and the same two hairstyles were constantly rerun. In the northern part imitating my sister, my inherent playmate. I walked the narrow stairs of a country church tower to visit the witch on Halloween night...shaking in her inordinate power. At my grandparent's home, and at the end of a long tiring day, we spoke of relatives who lived far away. And, we talked of things that were yet to come as we watched the sinking of the Louisiana sun. Words settled over us like sleeping pills as we hypnotically gazed at the moonlit hills. We shelled purple hulled peas in that special little town until our fingers were dyed and sore. Then we sank gratefully into our hot feather mattresses at the end of the day to wake in the morning damp from the night's humid air.

Printed in the United States
by Baker & Taylor Publisher Services